AWAY IN
Deepwater

BOOK 3

CHRISTMAS
STOCKING
SWEETHEARTS

SARAH LAMB

A thank you to my proofreader, Brooke, and all of the lovely women who help ARC read to catch those typos I miss!

This book was not written by AI. Any typos are proudly (and embarrassingly!) my own human created ones!

ISBN paperback: ISBN: 978-1-960418-31-9

ISBN Large Print: ISBN: 978-1-960418-32-6

Cover © Charlene Raddon, https://silversagebookcovers.com

Excerpt: Holly in His Heart by Jo-Ann Roberts- Christmas Stocking Sweethearts Series Book 4

Copyright © 2024 J-Ann Roberts

Contents

To the lovely women over at Petticoats and Pistols, both authors and readers alike, who have accepted me into their wonderful group. I appreciate each of you.

Chapter 1

1870s, Virginia

The large ballroom filled with applause, and Samantha Lundy clasped her hands to her heart, then blew a kiss to the crowd of almost a hundred guests. Instantly, she was swarmed by men and women alike in their fancy evening clothes.

"My dear, you were magnificent," Mrs. Lydell, the party's hostess, said. "I am delighted you agreed to perform for us. I never tire of your voice."

"Such talent," another well-wisher said, and for a few moments, Samantha smiled, and thanked one person after the next. Eventually, the orchestra situated near the enormous Christmas tree covered in glass balls struck up a tune, and the guests returned to dancing.

She slipped down the hallway, past greenery and bows welcoming the Christmas season, quite truthfully relieved to be escaping the crush of people. The room had been overwhelmingly stifling, but it was her job to perform, and an opportunity afforded to few. She was grateful, of course, but Samantha had never cared for crowds or for being stared at. It took quite a bit of courage for her, and a great deal of practice, to get slightly more comfortable with singing before so many.

She turned down a hallway, and entered the room she'd been given to freshen up in. Once safely inside, she closed the door behind her and dropped into a plush chair, letting one hand brush over the deep purple upholstery.

When she'd arrived nearly four hours ago, Samantha hadn't had time for more than just the briefest of looks, as she'd arrived a little late, due to a transportation issue. Now, she couldn't help but marvel at how richly decorated this room was—just like each had been that she'd passed tonight.

No matter how many wealthy men and women she had performed for, Samantha had never stopped being impressed, and perhaps just a little surprised, at the elaborate displays of wealth some showed.

This room had the largest mirror Samantha had ever seen. It took up nearly half a wall. The furniture was incredibly ornate, and small landscapes framed in golden frames dotted the walls, against a brocade wallpaper. The Lydells were one of the wealthiest families in Virginia, so that was to be expected. Their house was so large, and staffed by so many servants, Samantha couldn't even imagine such a thing. Their teenage daughters wore jewels that likely cost more than her impressive fee to sing had. Their gowns were also likely worn only once, and also ridiculously expensive.

It was a very different experience from her own teenage years. She'd grown up often hungry, and never in anything beyond a simple work dress. She had never imagined she'd have dresses such as the beautiful and well-fitting red silk one she now wore.

Samantha stood, and checked her appearance in the oversized mirror, brushing back a few loose strands of her dark hair. Though she was leaving, she needed to look her best in case a guest of the party came across her. A yawn escaped, and she couldn't help but long for her bed. This was the third event of the week at which she'd performed until the early hours. It was difficult, but she was in demand, Steven had said. She must perform. It would be a shame to waste her talent.

Not only that, but the audience could be fickle. If she refused their requests, they would find someone else to patronize. Samantha had the dream of helping others one day, and to do that it took funds.

She had always loved music, and she was grateful to earn her living by sharing that talent with others. Lessons as a child had been a bright spot in her life, provided for several years by a talented music teacher named Melody Nightingale. The name had suited her teacher, and her kindness and obvious love for all things music had been shared by Samantha, until her family had been forced to move away for her father's work.

Samantha hadn't wanted to leave. In fact, she'd felt a terrible sense of fear about the entire thing, even if both her parents and Miss Nightingale had assured her she'd settle in and love her new home.

At first, she had. However, unfortunately, things hadn't gone at all like they had hoped, and it caused the almost painfully shy girl to grow up faster than she'd have wanted, and without the security of a loving family.

The first few months in Virginia had gone well enough. Then, it had all gone downhill from there, as first one, then the other of her parents had passed away from illness, leaving her alone and penniless at the age of seventeen. Samantha had taken a spot as a governess, as she was quite educated herself. There, she taught a young girl, and discovered the child had a gift for music. Samantha drew upon her past musical training to teach the girl, and found she enjoyed giving lessons and learning more about the world of music herself.

It was a few years later, while performing a song with the girl at one of her parents' parties, that she'd caught the eye of someone and her life changed. Now, she had enough money to care for all of her needs.

All thanks to Steven.

Her lips curved into a content smile, and her heart beat quicker at his name. Her fiancé, so tall and handsome, had given her more than the chance to provide for herself and keep music alive in her soul. He had given her the dream she'd always longed for. To make others feel, through music.

Steven was thirty-two, and a little older than her twenty-four, but he assured her none of that mattered to him. Indeed, it didn't to her. Steven had saved her in every way imaginable, and she felt nothing but love and gratitude toward him.

He'd provided additional lessons for her, helped her get the dresses she needed, taught her how to act genteel, and then started to find places for her to perform at.

Of course, as he'd paid for so much at first, she willingly let him handle her finances, and keep a portion for himself to reimburse him for the work he put in. Samantha wasn't quite sure how much she had, other than what was in a small bank account in her name, but whenever she wished for something, he got it for her, so she must have a good deal. He was keeping it safe for her, he'd promised the time or two she'd asked.

And, he reminded her, it had been rather expensive to give her all she needed, including new dresses to perform in so often. So, it was simply better he handle the financial aspect, both to compensate himself and to make sure she wasn't taken advantage of.

Another yawn escaped, and Samantha headed toward the door. She couldn't wait to get home. Three late nights this week had been one too many.

Steven would be waiting to escort her out. She just needed to find her way to the door that would lead directly to the carriage she'd arrived in. Though she was an esteemed performer, she was also that, and not a guest, meaning she wasn't allowed to enter or depart through the front.

Samantha left the room, and tilted her head, smiling at the music being played. Mozart. She loved his arias. They were difficult to perform, but how she loved them!

She turned left, and then right, and paused, hearing voices. When she realized one was Steven's, she picked up her skirts to hurry toward him, then froze as his words met her ears.

"You shouldn't be here. I told you to stay away."

Samantha hesitated. Steven sounded upset, and she didn't want to interrupt.

"But you're gone so much," a woman's voice said, desperation in her tone. "Have you forgotten about me?"

Stiffening, Samantha felt a sickening jolt in her stomach and pressed one hand to it. Who was her fiancé talking to?

"Marta, you know why I'm doing this. It's for us. I'm going to stay with Samantha as long as her beauty and her voice lasts, and take my well-deserved cut of her earnings. You know money's been difficult. You really want me to give all of that up? For *us* to give all of that up?"

Samantha's head felt light, and her legs threatened to give out. What was she overhearing? She took a stumbling step forward, then another. She wasn't far from the corner of the hallway, where, if she turned, she was sure to see him, and whoever he was talking to.

Her hands trembled, and she squeezed them into fists. Marta. Who was she? How long had Steven been playing her false? Had the other woman been before her or after?

"But I'm your wife!" the other woman protested.

Samantha gasped loudly. And then backed away as Steven rushed around the corner and nearly knocked her over. His face was one of anger. Then, it smoothed quickly when he saw her. He reached for her hand. "Darling, there you are."

"No, stay away," Samantha whispered, shaking her head frantically. "I heard. I heard it all. You're married and only using me for what I can make you." Her voice caught on the last words, and a sob escaped.

The other woman hadn't appeared. She'd likely run away, but Samantha didn't care. Didn't want to see her. Didn't even want to see Steven right now. She felt confused. Hurt. And hoped what she'd overheard had been a mistake, but her instinct told her it wasn't.

Steven's eyes narrowed at her, and then he crossed his arms over his chest and laughed as though she'd told him something incredibly hilarious.

"And what will you do about it?" he asked her.

She looked into his handsome face. The dark curls of his hair, the deep blue eyes, and the fine chiseled features. Ones she'd thought belonged to her.

"People will talk," he continued, his voice low, though it dripped with sarcasm and coolness. "But it won't be about me. They'll talk about the poor, desperate woman who wanted so badly to be a singer, to move into the higher levels of society, that she threw herself at anyone...including a married man, and didn't care."

"But...but..." Samantha's words wouldn't escape. They felt trapped, as she did here, in this hallway.

"But your manager, who helped you, raised you up, a good, honest man, had no idea of your misguided affection. He will be blameless. You...will not be." Steven's eyes, ones she'd once loved looking into, burned her with their coldness.

It was a lie, all of it. She was innocent. But she also knew what he said was the truth. It was not him who would be blamed. It would be her.

Steven's lips curled into a smile. "Unless."

"Unless what?" she whispered.

"Unless you do just what I say," he told her, "and keep singing. Keep making me money. Because if you don't, then I will tell everyone, and it will ruin you."

"It will ruin you as well," Samantha whispered hoarsely. "You wouldn't dare."

"You forget who has control over all of your money," Steven replied, an expression of delight on his face. "It's enough to keep me well off for quite some time. I'm afraid, my dear, you have no other option."

Samantha stood there shaking as Steven turned and started down the hallway. He glanced over his shoulder only once. "Are you coming?" he asked, as though this had been a normal conversation. "The carriage is waiting."

Wordlessly, her legs followed of their own accord, however, her mind was frantically trying to find a solution. She knew she'd never do what he asked. Would never risk scandal. Not only would it ruin her reputation, but it wouldn't be the truth, and above all else, Samantha was a firm believer in being true. To others, and to oneself.

On the carriage ride back to her small townhome, Samantha sat still, quiet, and looking through the window. Festive Christmas decorations adorned each shop window, and the front of many homes. Normally, she'd be admiring their beauty, but right now, Samantha was still upset.

She didn't say a thing as she entered her home alone, turned the lock behind her, and did the only thing she knew to do.

Raced to her bedroom to pack.

Chapter 2

Deepwater, Missouri

Even though it was cold outside, Dirk Schmidt was quite warm, even almost hot, as he spread the ink on the typeset letters, then cranked the handle on his printing press. With a grunt, he applied the extra weight from the platen by pulling on another handle.

He'd been at this for almost two hours, creating the town's newspaper. After everything had been properly typeset—a task that had been done the previous day—he'd started to create the paper. Once the ink had dried fully, he'd flip the paper over—upside down and backwards—and print it again, making the four-page newspaper.

He paused and rubbed at his shoulder, then pulled the paper free to inspect it. It looked good. Though he had a few more he needed to do, Dirk thought he could take just a moment's break before finishing the newspaper, and then printing the advertisements the general store wanted.

His stomach chose that moment to remind him it was well past lunchtime. Dirk walked upstairs to his living quarters over the shop, intending to grab a bite, then groaned. The fire had gone out in his small stove, and the beans he'd set there to cook had not. He was out of bread, but for a small heel, and had run out of butter and cheese as well. It had been a busy week, and his usual shopping trip had been postponed.

"The café it is," he decided, as he stoked the stove and hoped the fire wouldn't go out again. It had been his fault. If he'd taken a break to add more fuel to the fire, it wouldn't have died out.

Dirk went back down the stairs, grabbed his heavy coat, and walked out into the bleak day. The sky was gray, and the clouds spoke of long overdue snow. He hoped it would hold off at least until he'd eaten and was back home. Dirk's chilled body pushed him to hurry the few doors over to Maggie's Café.

Run by Maggie, of course, and her husband Hank, when he wasn't managing the livery he owned, the café was not only a place always ready to give a soul a nourishing meal, but also was the only such place in town.

When Dirk pushed open the café door, the small bell hanging above it rang out, and Maggie's head popped out from the kitchen. "Make yourself comfortable," she called. "I'll be right out."

Dirk nodded, and took a seat in one of the chairs near the crackling fireplace. He enjoyed sitting here and watching the flames, lost in his thoughts, or else reading one of the books Maggie kept there.

"What can I get you?" Maggie asked.

"Anything," Dirk said. "Whatever you have is fine by me."

"I'll be right back," she told him, and a moment later set down a tray with a bowl of beef stew, several rolls with a ball of butter, and a steaming cup of her cider.

"Looks good. Thank you," Dirk told her. "I was so busy working on the newspaper, I lost track of time and my stove went out. My intended lunch will now be my dinner," he laughed.

Maggie joined him in the laughter. "That'll happen when you forget to feed the flames," she agreed. "Anything good in the news?"

"You'll have to wait, just like everyone else." He winked.

"Have you started working on the special issue yet?" Maggie asked eagerly.

The special issue was the idea of the postmaster Peter, and his wife, Alyssa. They'd had the idea to invite each townsperson to submit a small story or poem, or even a thoughtful wish for the holiday season, so that everyone in town might enjoy it together as they sat in their homes on Christmas Day. The two were very encouraging of anything that had to do with providing means for others to enjoy stories, and had even donated the money to pay for the ink and the paper. Dirk himself was donating his time.

Everyone was excited about the special edition, and the fact it would actually be turned into a small book. Schoolchildren had labored over poems, jokes, riddles, and short stories. Adults had done the same, along with messages of encouragement and Christmas wishes. Even Dirk had done one.

"I'll be starting on it once I've gotten the newspaper finished, and an order for some flyers," Dirk assured her. "I think there might still be a few things to get to me. It looks like it's to be a nice, thick booklet when it's all done. I expect at least twenty-five pages, maybe more, depending on what else makes its way to me."

"How wonderful," Maggie said. "If you've any extras, bring them to the café. I'll put them on the shelves, next to the books."

Dirk nodded his agreement as Maggie walked away, allowing him to start his meal in quiet. The stew was just what he needed. Hearty, filling, warm. He ate spoonful after spoonful, until he realized he'd finished it.

Maggie, having some sort of sense about her customers when they were still hungry, came out of her kitchen with a slice of pound cake. "On the house," she said. "The whole meal. Consider it a contribution toward the special edition."

"Thank you," Dirk told her.

"I get the first copy?" she asked.

He laughed. "I'll see what I can do," he promised.

She returned to her kitchen with a satisfied expression on her face, and once the cake had been finished to the last crumb, Dirk stood to leave, his stomach now happy. When he stepped outside, the wind gusted so hard he had to pull his coat around him tightly.

Dirk trudged up the street toward the shop. He passed the empty building next to his. A year before, he'd bought the building, thinking perhaps he could expand his print shop by cutting through the wall since the buildings shared a wall. Upon further inspection, he'd realized it wouldn't work at all, and it had been sitting empty ever since.

Recently, he'd put an ad into a few papers, and hoped someone would come and rent it, either to become a business there in Deepwater, or else to live in, as either would be possible.

Perhaps it would even be a young couple. The place was big enough for two. The thought made him sigh, as he pushed open the door to his shop and hung his coat on a peg near the door.

He'd once had dreams of a future with someone. It hadn't worked out, and he'd likely missed his opportunity for a family of his own, but he didn't begrudge anyone a chance at love. Over the last five years, he'd kept to himself, determined never to fall in love again.

But maybe the holiday season, or the fact he was getting older and a little lonely, had softened him, and Dirk wondered if he'd ever meet the right woman for him. One who truly loved him for himself—not what he provided.

Deepwater had a way of bringing people in, people who were meant to be there, either for themselves or for others. Maybe he'd be so fortunate. And then again, maybe not.

Dirk bent over to pick up a scrap of paper that had fluttered down when he'd entered, bringing some of the wind with him. It was from the stack of notes from the schoolchildren. He glanced at it, and then the strangest tingle zipped through his fingers while goosebumps went over his arms.

The note read, simply, "You will find all you dream of."

He swallowed hard, then tossed the note on the table. "A child's wish," he said. "Nothing more."

But several more times that day, Dirk's eyes roamed to the scrap of paper, and the words seemed to echo in his mind. He wondered, was it possible? Would a Christmas wish come true for him?

Chapter 3

"Deepwater!" the driver's deep voice called, and the stagecoach slowed, then shuddered to a stop. Samantha looked around slowly as the door opened and the passengers disembarked.

"We leave in thirty-five minutes," the driver called, grunting as he wrestled with the bags of those who would stay on. "Be back here or catch the next if there's room. I've a schedule to keep, and I'm not waiting for anyone."

The majority of the passengers rushed toward a building with a sign proclaiming it was a café. Samantha patiently waited until it was her turn to point at the luggage. Only one other person looked to be staying, and they hurried away with just a small bag. As the driver set her things down, a man approached.

"Miss Lundy?" he asked.

"Yes. Mr. Schmidt?" Samantha paused from where she had been brushing the dust off her skirt. It didn't matter it was December. The town hadn't had snow recently, and it was as dry and as dusty as she'd imagined the place to be. It had been her experience that the towns with the nicest of names usually suffered from wishful thinking.

"Indeed. Let me help with your bags, and I'll show you to your house. Well, that is, if you want it." He stepped forward, and picked up her heavy trunk.

Samantha was about to protest, but he lifted it so effortlessly, all she could do was snap her mouth shut and pick up her two bags, following him a short distance away.

Mr. Schmidt set her trunk down in front of a small but neat-looking building tucked between two others, then opened the door. "Glad to have someone here to care for the place," he said, swinging the door open.

Samantha followed him inside, glancing around curiously. The last week had felt both incredibly slow-moving, and too fast for her to comprehend.

After the night she'd discovered her fiancé had not only been using her for what she could give him, but that he was also married, she'd packed all she could into her travel trunk and two bags. The following morning, she'd had her things taken to the train station and had secured a rail ticket. A discarded newspaper had caught her eye, and for some reason there was a small map of Missouri. A town, one that had recently gotten its own stage stop, evidently was large enough to make the news. Deepwater, it was called.

She'd made arrangements to get there at once. Any Western town able to get a mention in a Virginia newspaper must be large enough to hide in and not draw attention.

However, once she arrived here, she saw that was as far from the truth as possible. Deepwater was tiny. Samantha squeezed her larger carpetbag tightly, and wondered if the town even had a bank. She'd withdrawn all of her money on her way to the train station, and had hardly slept for the last week, as she'd transferred from train to train, and finally to a cramped stagecoach.

"I hope it will do," Mr. Schmidt said, and Samantha startled, realizing that she'd roamed the entire house, yet not even seen anything within it, she was so lost in her thoughts.

"It will," she answered, giving him a bright smile. "I'll take it. It's very fortunate that you have this place for me to rent. I'm so glad I saw the newspaper ad you placed at one of the stage stops. I apologize for assuming you would still have this place—and accept my tenancy—but I'm grateful you are considering it."

"As long as it's suitable," he said, "it's yours. I don't want you to take it if you don't care for it. The café has rooms for rent until something else opens, but I'll be honest in the fact that Deepwater doesn't usually have too many vacancies," he explained. "Most newcomers build a home, though this isn't exactly the best time of year for that."

"This will do nicely," Samantha said, turning around the main room. "Thank you."

Mr. Schmdit nodded. "I've the place next door, so should you need anything, you can let me know. Rent's due the first of the month."

Samantha nodded. "Speaking of money, is there a bank in town?"

"There is," he said, and pointed. "That building with the dark green door."

"Thank you," she told him again. "I appreciate your help, and the place to call home."

He looked at her curiously. "What brings you to Deepwater? Do you have family here? I don't recognize your last name."

She hesitated. "No. I do not." Her fingers twisted, despite her determination to remain calm. "I was looking for a change. A fresh start."

He nodded. "Deepwater is good for that. A lot of folks here came looking for the same, and now call it home."

"Good. Then I'm sure it will happen for me as well." Samantha smiled, though she didn't feel it.

She didn't want to be rude, but her trip had been long, and she longed for nothing more than a good scrub. It was nothing short of a miracle the place was partially furnished, and with a stove. She'd be able to heat water, at least.

"One last question," she said. "Where can I go for furniture?"

"You've nothing coming in?" he asked.

She shook her head no.

"The general store has some. I don't know what all they've got, though," he told her.

"That's fine. Once I've washed up and changed into something clean, I'll go and inquire."

He took a step toward the door. "Just let me know if you need anything."

Samantha thanked him, and closed the door. She turned to the kitchen area of the home and was grateful that Mr. Schmidt had a small fire burning. She heated water in the battered kettle he left behind so that she could clean as much of the travel off of her as possible, and an hour later, feeling refreshed, left her new home, setting out for the bank.

The bank owner hadn't asked any questions, and had taken her large deposit. Samantha had felt the need to explain herself, not wanting to be mistaken for a criminal, so she simply told him she was starting over after the loss of a loved one. It was true, really. She had lost Steven, and she had loved him. But her loss was likely a blessing.

It was just upsetting that along with the loss of him, she'd lost her love for music. What once brought her endless happiness, a joy like no other, she now never wanted to partake in again.

Samantha placed her order in the general store for modest furniture to be delivered as soon as possible. Then, quite hungry, she made her way to the café.

As the door pushed open and glorious warmth rushed to her, Samantha closed her eyes for a moment. This place had a good feel about it. It wasn't just the warmth or the smell of baking bread. The woman standing behind the long counter also felt welcoming.

"Hello, dear," the woman said. "New to town?"

"Yes," Samantha said. "I'm hoping to get a meal here. I'm not set up yet to cook."

"Of course. You've a choice of potato and corn stew or chicken and dumplings."

"The stew, please," she said, and sat down.

A few moments later, a steaming bowl of stew, a thick slab of bread with butter, and a cup of tea were placed before her.

"Here you are," the woman told her. "I'm Maggie, and this is my café. If you need anything else, you just let me know."

"Thank you, Maggie," Samantha said, picking up her spoon.

"I don't recognize your accent. Where are you from?" the café owner asked.

Samantha hesitated, then said, "Virginia."

"Got family nearby?"

"No," Samantha answered, regretting her decision to come. She just wanted to eat her meal in peace and stay in her home, away from everyone and everything. Perhaps she'd chosen poorly, moving here. The people were a little too inquisitive.

When she saw Maggie still looking at her, she brought her spoon to her lips and said, "I just wanted a chance to get away for a while."

The other woman nodded, a thoughtful look on her face. "Deepwater's good for that," she said.

The café door's bell rang just then, and Maggie turned away to greet the couple who had just walked in.

Samantha ate, and had no complaints about the food. It was simple, but some of the best she'd ever had. Her eyes took in the small town before her. A worry filled her, and Samantha hoped it wouldn't grow into a truth.

With Deepwater being so small, even though she'd taken precautions, what if Steven were to find where she was and come to drag her back? With so few people, there was nowhere to hide.

She'd need to keep to herself. Not share anything more than she had. If she did, it would make it all the easier for him to find her—and potentially ruin her life.

Chapter 4

Hands on hips, Dirk nodded in satisfaction at the stack of pages printed before him. Soon, he'd begin the slow task of cutting and binding the small books. Alyssa, the postmaster's wife, was a very talented artist, and had drawn a lovely sketch for the cover. It had been carved onto a block by a local woodcarver, and that was then inked after it was placed into the proper place on the printing press to make it part of the newspaper.

Though it would be a long task, sewing together the spine of each book by hand, Dirk didn't mind. After all, it was his way of contributing. The general store had given him several spools of a thick red thread, and he'd use that so there was a little color on the edge.

The clock in the room chimed the hour, and Dirk reached for his jacket. Today was mail delivery, and he always looked forward to stopping over at the post office. Even if he didn't receive anything himself, it was nice to visit with Peter or Alyssa for a moment, along with anyone else who happened to be there, also seeking their mail.

The short walk was brisk. It felt like snow was in the air. They could use a little more than the dusting they'd gotten overnight. Christmas was only a few weeks away, and there was nothing so pretty, nor so magical, as snow at Christmas. It made winter feel peaceful, cozy even. Gave the eye something new to look at other than bare trees and brown grass.

A small crowd was gathered in front of the post office window, and Dirk waited patiently for his turn. Snippets of conversations reached his ears from those around him, but nothing really caught his attention, until he heard a woman ask, "Why do you think that Miss Lundy keeps to herself so?"

Miss Lundy. There was a woman he'd thought about more than once since she'd moved into the place next door. He hadn't seen who'd asked the question, but they were right. Miss Lundy kept to herself, rarely doing more than church, a quick stop at the café, or the general store. As far as he knew, she never even went to the post office, which Dirk found odd. Everyone looked forward to the twice-weekly news that might arrive for them.

The line shuffled forward again, and he was at the front.

"Hello, Dirk," Peter said. "Got a package, and it might be for you."

"For me?" Dirk asked.

"Well, it's got your old address on there, anyway. The name's all smudged, so I can't make it out. See an S pretty clearly, so I was thinking it's for you? If it's not, bring it back to me," Peter told him.

"I will," Dirk said, accepting the small bundle.

He set off toward his shop, curious about what was inside, and who the sender could be. There was a name in the return corner, but he didn't recognize it. It simply said Melody Nightingale. As far as he could recall, he didn't know anyone by that name.

Dirk threw open the door to his shop and rubbed his hands together to warm them before he stared at the package again. Without even waiting to take off his coat, he pulled one edge of the package open. A letter dropped out. Wondering if it might give more details, he unfolded it, and started to read. The paper was unusual. It was a piece of sheet music. Puzzled, he turned it over, and saw:

My dear Samantha,

As I write this...

Samantha. Samantha? Oh! Dirk realized suddenly. Miss Lundy. This must be for her. He hurriedly put the letter back inside of the package, then left his shop again, glad he was already in his jacket.

Taking the few steps to the house next door, he knocked twice and waited. It was so cold out, the air from his nostrils looked like smoke puffing out. Luckily, the door opened just a moment later. Dirk tried to ignore the sudden tightness in this throat as he beheld Miss Lundy, for there was no other phrase to describe the beauty before him.

Her hair was pinned back, but dark, loose tendrils framed her face. Her dress was the color of the sapphire necklace his granny had, and it complimented her fair skin.

"Mr. Schmidt," she said. "Hello."

Near dumbstruck, Dirk swallowed hard. "I, uh, got a package that was meant for you," he said. "Apologies. I opened it. But I stopped reading the letter the second I saw your name."

It might have been his imagination, but her face went even paler, as she reached forward to take the bundle. Dirk noticed her hand tremble slightly, which he thought was unusual, but her shoulders suddenly sagged in relief as she gasped, "Oh! It's from Melody Nightingale. I'd recognize that handwriting anywhere. But how odd!"

Her smile returned to her face again, and she said, "Thank you for bringing this to me. I've no idea what it is, but I do hope it wasn't any trouble for you."

"None at all," he assured her.

"Where are my manners?" she asked, with a shake of her head. "Please come in from the cold. Can I offer you some tea? A slice of crumb cake?"

His stomach embarrassed him just then by grumbling, and Miss Lundy couldn't hide her small laugh.

"I think that's a yes?" she teased.

"Thank you," he mumbled, hoping his face wasn't too red.

Dirk followed her in and then shut the door. Miss Lundy had made the place very cozy indeed. A carpet had been laid down in the center of the large room, and a small sofa and two small chairs were nearby a table and the fireplace.

"It looks nice," he told her, sitting in one of the chairs.

"Eventually, I'll get a few paintings for the wall," Miss Lundy told him. "I understand Alyssa, who I only met once, is a talented artist. I think I'd like to commission her, and have something custom painted."

"She's real talented, Miss Lundy," Dirk assured her. "She's even made the artwork for the Christmas booklet I'm putting together for the town."

"Tell me about that," Miss Lundy said. "Right after you agree to call me Samantha."

Now Dirk was sure there was no hiding the heat that had rushed to his face. "Samantha," he repeated. "And call me Dirk, please. Everyone does."

"I will," she said, bringing over two cups of tea and two slices of cake.

Dirk spent the next half hour explaining to her about the book the town was making, and how once everything had been printed, he'd sew it together. She asked questions about his press, and he was delighted when Samantha asked if she could see him use it sometime.

He readily agreed, and before he knew it, an hour had passed, and he hastily excused himself, apologizing for staying so long.

"I didn't mind at all," Samantha said. "Thank you for the invitation to see your print shop. I will take you up on that soon."

Dirk nodded, and waved as he stepped back out into the cold. He marveled at how quickly Samantha had seemed to settle into her new home, but the woman's comments at the post office line came back to mind. Samantha did seem to keep to herself. He wondered why that was, but perhaps there had been a clue, when he'd watched her place the package on a corner table for later.

First there had been fear, and then a great sadness before she'd seen the sender. Dirk knew that feeling. He'd experienced it himself years before. Her eyes were those of someone who had been deeply betrayed by a person she loved.

Chapter 5

"Miss Lundy! Miss Lundy!"

Samantha cringed as she stilled, then forced her grimace into a pleasant expression as she turned around. Immediately, she felt bad. The townsfolk had been nothing but welcoming. Perhaps...too welcoming. With the exception of her recent visit with Dirk, she'd tried to avoid too much contact with others, and honestly wasn't quite sure why she'd even invited him in and spent so long talking to him.

There was just something about Dirk...something that made her feel almost as though they were two of a kind. The idea was preposterous, of course. He was a printer.

She was a singer. Yet, there was just this feeling that he would understand, if he knew her story.

It was unlikely anyone else would. She almost hated to go into the café. Though Maggie had been nothing but kind, her questions bordered on prying.

The lovely pink-cheeked reverend's wife, Laura, was across the street and hurried over. "I just wanted to say hello," she said with a smile.

"It's Samantha," Samantha said with a smile of her own. This one was genuine. For some reason, both the reverend and his wife radiated goodness, but not in the false way some did. She felt so much better when she was around them. They were different from what she'd have expected a reverend and his wife to be. Gabriel cracked jokes and told stories from the front of the church that had those listening in fits of laughter. Laura chattered away, was the local school teacher, and seemed to possess a sharp intellect.

Over one of their cups of tea, Samantha had asked Dirk about them, and had been shocked to learn Gabriel hadn't always been a pastor, and that he'd had *quite* a different past. Laura, Dirk had told her, had arrived in Deepwater when the stagecoach she'd been traveling on broke down. She had been an instrumental part of helping save their town from a criminal.

Each story he'd told her was more incredible than the next, and she was in awe of some of the people here.

Including the fact, she wasn't the first to use Deepwater as a hiding place—not that she'd tell anyone that was why she was here.

"I wanted to know how you'd been settling in," Laura asked.

"Everyone has been perfectly wonderful," Samantha said truthfully, "and I enjoy the town. I've never been to a place before where everyone is so friendly and welcoming, almost to a fault."

Laura laughed again. "I'm sure you are glad that you chose this town to move to."

"If I am being honest," Samantha said slowly, "I just chose this town by chance. It wasn't really planned."

"Then you were perhaps meant to be here," Laura said. "Led to this place and its people for a reason. Deepwater has been helpful and healing for many. I hope you find that as well."

"I do too," Samantha said softly. If only that would happen. She'd never wish for anything else again.

Laura kindly changed the subject. "I stopped you because I have a question. We are putting on a Christmas program at the church on Christmas Eve," Laura told her. "I'm looking for a few more people to put on some sort of performance."

Samantha's chest tightened. Had someone found out she sang? Perhaps had even discovered who she was? She had no illusions after her quiet two weeks here in Deepwater that she was completely safe and Steven wouldn't find her. Not if he wanted her to make him more money. Steven was determined, and had a wide reach. It was possible someone at the train station told him which direction she'd gone, and it was without a doubt that the man at the bank had told him she'd withdrawn every cent she owned under her name.

Deepwater also hadn't been quite as secluded as she'd imagined. She couldn't walk down the street without everyone waving or calling hello. There were some—like Dirk and Laura—whom she thought she'd enjoy the company of. Others, she wasn't sure.

"That is, if you'd be willing," Laura continued. The woman, who was only a little older than her, laughed, and the sound was a lovely tinkling. "Not everyone can sing or wants to. A few people are reading poems. We have someone playing the harmonica, another a fiddle. Any talent at all is welcome," she added. "Even if you aren't especially gifted in any capacity! We just need more people to make it a proper program."

Samantha relaxed. It was just a general invitation. Not because they knew who she was.

"I appreciate the invitation," she answered. "May I think on it? I'm not very comfortable with the idea of performing."

"Then you won't," Laura said firmly. "We don't want you to do it unless you want to. Just know if you change your mind, you will be welcome." She reached over and squeezed Samantha's hands. "I'm so glad you are here, and I hope we will become good friends."

"I hope so too," Samantha said, a little surprised to realize that she meant it. Then, she noticed Laura's arms. Each had a heavy-looking basket on it. "Let me help you," she offered. "Where are you going?"

"To the church," Laura said gratefully, handing Samantha one of the baskets. "I always carry our groceries myself, instead of getting them delivered, but today was the day I ended up with more than I could comfortably lift."

They walked together, and Laura kept the conversation flowing the entire time. When they arrived, Laura thanked her as she took the basket from Samantha.

Samantha turned to leave when she heard piano music. She paused, cocking her head. Laura had left, and no one was around to see her. The song was one she knew. One she'd performed many times and loved.

To her surprise, as her eyes sought the pianist, she saw it was Dirk! His own eyes were closed as his fingers flew over the keys, and he bowed his head low, also obviously feeling each note within him deeply. He was the last person she'd expected to be playing so beautifully, but as the song's intensity grew, Samantha found herself transported in time, back to the first evening she'd performed this song.

Her stomach swirled with a mixture of longing and excitement as she followed along with the notes. Though she hadn't dared admit it to anyone, not even herself until now, she really did miss performing. It wasn't about the praise from the audience. She really didn't care about that. It was the feeling of joy that filled her when she heard the music and sang, and how she tried to project her emotions of the song into the audience.

Nothing had moved her to tears the way it had to see her songs do the same for her audience. She listened as the music reached its crescendo, and then slowed, before fading away. As the last notes sounded, Samantha realized tears were falling down her cheeks.

Wiping them away with the back of one hand, she walked as quickly as she could back to her home. As soon as she opened the door, Samantha rushed inside, then shut it behind her and leaned against the wooden frame.

Could she not escape music anywhere? Even her old music teacher had found her. Her eyes fell to the Christmas stocking that had been inside of the package Dirk had gotten by mistake. A beautiful deep blue with silver stitching, silver stars, and a nightingale had been sewn onto it. A reminder of both of Miss Nightingale, and the music she made and created for others.

Hesitating a moment, Samantha made her way over to the letter from her former teacher, that she'd tucked inside the stocking. Once more, she read it.

My dear Samantha,

As I write this, I can almost hear your sweet voice singing the special version of this carol you created so long ago. I hope this stocking finds you well and happy, your voice still bringing joy to all who hear it.

May this stocking remind you of the music we shared, and of the teacher who always believed in your unique voice—both at the piano and in song. Keep it as a reminder of me, or give it away in order to spread joy to others around you. Either outcome will make me equally happy.

You will always have a special place in my heart, and in the music of Nightingale.

With warmest regards,

Melody Nightingale

Samantha closed her eyes for a moment as she refolded the letter, and placed it upon the mantel. She had been fortunate to meet Miss Nightingale. Though she hadn't had lessons for long, they had been what had helped her to get started, first teaching music to a private pupil as her governess, then performing with her at one of her pupil's parents' gatherings, and being seen by the man who she thought loved her, and who elevated her status far beyond what she she'd ever have been able to achieve on her own.

It had been a surprise to receive the stocking from her old music teacher. As had the letter had been.

Samantha wondered how the woman had known where to find her. If Miss Nightingale had, did that mean she hadn't covered her tracks well at all? Would Steven find her soon too?

She wasn't sure. Samantha only felt peace at the idea her old teacher found her, and decided that it was something akin to Christmas magic. That must be it.

However, seeing the stocking also filled her with determination. After hearing Dirk's beautiful music, Samantha had made up her mind. She and music? They were no longer to be companions. She'd keep the stocking visible as a reminder that her time singing for others—and herself—had passed.

And she'd continue to pray Steven would never find her.

Chapter 6

The snow fell outside of the window. Fat, icy flakes stuck to the glass pane and collected near the edge of the window's frame. A movement outside caught Dirk's eye, and he was surprised to see Samantha stop in front of his door and raise her hand as if to knock.

A moment later, the sound met his ears, and Dirk hurried over to let her inside. "Hello," he told her. He stepped backward, and gestured, inviting her in. "What brings you out in this weather?"

"I have your rent," Samantha said, stepping inside and glancing around curiously. "I hoped to see your shop as well, if the time suits you."

"Of course," Dirk said, trying not to stammer. He tried to calm himself, hardly able to believe she really had come to see his shop, and had not merely been polite.

Samantha glanced at the stack of the Christmas booklet papers he'd finished cutting out. Each page was in its own pile. "My goodness, look at all of those! Is this for the book you are making?"

He nodded. "Sure is." Dirk grinned.

"No one else has seen it yet."

"I feel honored," she laughed, "and will not peek further, so I don't spoil my own surprise, since I assume I will also be able to have one?"

"You will," he told her. Then, he motioned around the shop. "Look around. Ask any questions."

Samantha nodded, and made a slow circle around his front room, looking at the small stacks of papers here and there he'd printed, and had ready for his various customers.

There were flyers, the upcoming town newspaper, and some sheet music Gabriel had requested. He watched as Samantha picked up one of the pages, and smiled at it. There was a faraway look in her eyes for a moment before she set it down. "You print most everything, don't you?" she asked, resuming her slow walk.

"If it's possible to print, I do," he told her. He led her to the large printing press. "This is where it happens. Once whatever I'm going to print is typeset—that means putting the letters into this frame which is then placed into the platen—I ink it carefully. Afterward, I put my paper into this holder, fold it down, crank this handle here, and move this lever, applying the pressure needed to ensure the ink takes to the page.

"Once it has sat for a moment, I reverse the process, and raise the paper holder to fetch out whatever it was I was printing. The paper gets set aside to dry. Depending on the ink, the drying time can vary. I like to be careful, and give it a little extra time, just to prevent the ink from smearing. I pride myself on the quality of my work." Dirk stopped suddenly, wondering if he'd perhaps bored her or talked too much. However, to his surprise, she was nodding, her full attention on his explanation.

"It's exemplary work," Samantha said, leaning forward to inspect the newspaper. "At times in Virginia, one could hardly make out sections of the news. It was printed so close it seemed there were no spaces between words. The ink would also run or be blurry. It was frustrating at times."

"That's the problem with some papers," Dirk agreed. "With the price of paper, to keep costs low, they often sacrifice quality. Such as you said, rushing or printing the words touching. Not here." He shook his head, and allowed the pride to creep into his voice. "Not in my shop."

"The town is lucky to have you," Samantha said.

Dirk felt his cheeks warm. "I've got to check the kettle," he told her. "Could I convince you to enjoy a cup of tea with me?"

"I'd be delighted," Samantha told him.

"You just keep looking around. I'll be back soon," Dirk told her, and went to his living quarters. His water was boiling, and he filled a teapot, set some of Maggie's special winter tea blend of cinnamon, lemon, and cloves to steep, and grabbed the best two mugs he owned.

Dirk couldn't help but feel just a little nervous. It had been a long time since he'd asked someone to share tea with him. Especially a woman. And most certainly not a woman as beautiful and smart as Samantha seemed to be. He welcomed her curiosity, and how genuine it was.

He returned with the tea, and the two sat at the small table he had in his front shop. Samantha shook her head as she gestured around the room. "This is really something! I had no idea how much effort went into printing, and after looking at what you've created, I can see that you put in more effort than most."

"I try to do the best that I can for others," Dirk told her honestly. "That's just the kind of person I am. Especially out here. We are a small town, and we don't have access to as many things as some of the larger towns do—especially those back East. But that doesn't mean we can't have pride in what we do create."

"You speak as though you aren't from here originally," Samantha said. She sat in one of his chairs.

"I'm not," he told her with a shrug. "Like a lot of others, I made my way here."

A thoughtful expression formed on her lovely face. "It seems that so many in this town have."

"It's filled with good people," Dirk said. "Some of the best I know."

"It seems it," Samantha agreed, sipping slowly from her mug. Then she asked, "What do you print the most of? The newspaper?"

"Yes, I think so, and as I'm the only printer for a few towns over, I get a lot of people coming to me for flyers and their towns' newspapers too. Truthfully, I've gotten so busy, I might need to hire a little help soon."

"If you need assistance with the book you are making for the town, let me know. If there is any way I can help with the binding of it, I'd be happy to," Samantha offered.

"I might just take you up on that," Dirk said. "I hope to have the final pages dry by tomorrow. Then, I can cut them, and the sorting and sewing can begin."

"Just the little bit I saw looked to be a wonderful assortment of pages," Samantha told him, rising from the table to look at his small stacks of the book.

Dirk joined her. "It is. We've got everything! Two short stories, several poems, a good number of jokes and riddles and wishes, and even a carol."

Samantha picked up the sheet music, "Away in a Manger." There was a strange look on her face that he couldn't decipher. "I always loved that song," she mused.

To Dirk's surprise, Samantha sang a few of the lines. Her voice was sweet and clear, and it was obvious to him that she'd had some sort of vocal training. He stared at her, mesmerized.

Samantha broke off mid verse, and set the page down. "I've a funny story about that song," she said, almost seeming to try and prevent him from talking.

"Is that so?" he asked.

Dirk knew he'd listen to any story she had to tell him. He'd listen to anything, story or not. He just wanted to be with her, spend time with her. There was a connection he felt, and he prayed it would grow. Now that Samantha Lundy had come into his life, Dirk didn't want her to leave.

"As a girl, I had music lessons," she told him, letting a finger run over the sheet music. "Though I was not the best at playing the piano, I could do a passable version of 'Away in a Manger.' Truthfully," she laughed, "it was the most recognizable of anything I learned. I was never able to play the piano as well as I liked. The melody, though..." The thoughtful look formed on her face again.

Samantha turned to him, almost sheepishly, and said, "You might laugh, but as I could play it, I'd copy the notes, but create my own lyrics, and give it to others as a gift."

"That's no different than a poem set to a familiar tune," Dirk assured her. He hesitated, then asked, "Do you still sing or play?"

A cloud formed over her face. "No," Samantha said, briskly. "My time for that is over."

He shouldn't push, Dirk knew he shouldn't. After all, he had his own reasons for keeping to himself, his own reasons for hiding his talents and no longer doing the things he loved. Still, the question burned in him.

"I hope you won't mind another question," he said, slowly. When she didn't answer, he continued, "Your voice is incredible. Why not offer it up to the town for the concert?"

"I told you. My time for singing is over." Samantha's jaw tensed, and she didn't meet his eyes.

"I'm sorry," Dirk said quietly. "I don't mean to upset you. It's just you've such a gift. Those few lines you sang..." He shook his head, "You've the voice of an angel. I've not heard that since—" He stopped, and amended, "Forgive me. I shouldn't pry."

"No, you shouldn't," Samantha said, her voice tight. "And though it seems the town is filled with people who say that, too many do."

"Now look, I've apologized," Dirk told her. His stomach sank. He wanted nothing more than to return to a few moments ago, before what he thought was a simple question had upset her so.

"I realize that," Samantha said. "I just..." She turned away, but not before Dirk saw tears forming, or heard the tremble in her voice.

Dirk was about to apologize again, when Samantha hurried over to the door of his shop. "Thank you for the tea," she told him. "Let me know when you need help with the books."

"Wait!" Dirk pleaded.

"I cannot have this conversation," Samantha told him tersely. "I came to Deepwater to escape. There. I've said it." She closed her eyes for a moment, and when she reopened them, they were pain-filled.

"I loved to sing. But it was taken from me in the sense that my gift, as everyone called it, felt dirty, soiled. I felt used. I cannot expect you to understand, but the fact remains, I will never sing again for anyone else."

Chapter 7

Samantha refused to let herself meet Dirk's eyes as she fled his shop. She rushed out so quickly, she wasn't even sure that she had closed the door fully.

The snow made her short walk slippery, but that didn't matter to her. She sought her shelter. Home. The four walls where she could be alone with her thoughts. Without anyone to betray her. Or anyone to get too close.

Samantha was grateful for the snow. It would keep people indoors until it had stopped. After all, it was several inches high right now, and made for treacherous travel.

Travel. Would Steven be traveling, seeking her? He had the means and the contacts to send someone else after her.

Perhaps that was the route he'd take. A private detective or a hired gun.

The idea made her shiver, even though her home was warm, and Samantha pulled the warm blanket that sat on her small sofa closer around her.

I just want to be safe.

The thought escaped. And it was true. That was what she wanted. But she wanted more. She wanted companionship. Wasn't that why she'd sought out Dirk? Someone to talk with?

But that couldn't be why she'd gone there. Nor was it because of her curiosity over his printing press. If she'd been curious, she wouldn't have gone now, today. If she'd simply wanted to chat with someone, she'd have visited Laura, or the café.

No, she'd wanted to be with Dirk, as foolish of an idea as that was.

Samantha sighed, and rubbed at her temples. What a fine mess she was in. She'd left Virginia to escape, protect her reputation, and here she was, entertaining the idea of a romantic attachment with a man again. What was she thinking?

It was obvious to her Dirk felt something between them as well. The way he looked at her. Smiled at her. Stood closely.

But he'd been a gentleman, through and through. Never pressed her, though they could have been considered in a compromising situation, being alone. He also never made her feel uncomfortable. In fact, it was the exact opposite. And it was for that very reason that Samantha found herself wanting to seek him out.

Fear had gotten in her way. Had led her to act how she just had. And pride would keep her from losing the man who treated her well, and who had the potential to become a good friend.

Samantha stood slowly from the sofa and refolded the blanket. She knew what she had to do. It didn't mean she liked the idea, but it was the right thing. Right didn't always mean easy, she'd often told her pupil when she'd been a governess. How right that was.

Bundling up once more, Samantha walked back to the print shop, then knocked. The door opened a moment later, and a surprised Dirk stared at her.

"I'm sorry," Samantha whispered. "Please, forgive me?"

He took her hands and pulled her into his shop, closing the door behind them gently. They stood for a long moment, simply looking at each other. Samantha realized one of Dirk's hands was still holding hers. But she didn't mind. It felt warm. Safe. Comforting.

He cleared his throat. "I understand, maybe more than you know, about running away from something. I also came to Deepwater to escape. And I...I..."

A heavy silence filled the room. Samantha watched as conflicting emotions warred on Dirk's face. A pang of regret filled her, as well as worry.

"Is there any tea left?" Samantha asked suddenly. "It's been my experience that sometimes the difficult stories are best told over tea."

"Yes. It's still warm," Dirk said, leading her back over to the table. He motioned for her to wait, then hurried upstairs, and then was back down a moment later, a tin of cookies from the general store in his hand.

Samantha accepted one, and poured them more tea. She studied him a moment as she slid his mug to him. "Well," she said lightly. "It seems we are both here, escaping someone or something. I admit, that makes me feel slightly better. Unless, of course, it turns out you are a hardened criminal." She arched a brow, trying not to let her lips twitch as she teased him.

Dirk laughed, which was what she was hoping to make him do. "Not a criminal," he said. "Just, a bit like you. The thing I loved—just as you said—grew soiled. Tainted."

"Do you want to talk about it?" Samantha asked. She raised her cup to her lips.

Dirk frowned, and then nodded. "I do want to tell you, because it relates, in a way, to your singing. And how you said you won't do it anymore."

Curious, she leaned forward slightly, waiting.

"I was a pianist, in Massachusetts. I've played since I was a boy. My family is filled with musicians. Piano was where my talent rested. I began to be hired to perform at gatherings."

Samantha nodded. She understood that very well. That was the world from which she'd come, as well. It did seem the two of them had much in common. She just hadn't ever expected to find that here, in this small town.

"Well," Dirk sighed, "that's where I met her. A stunning, talented woman, with a voice that could light up any room. Letta was her name. She sang, thrilling any audience before her. Letta was a few years older than me, but that didn't matter. I simply played, lending my skills to better enhance her performances."

When he grew quiet, Samantha rested her fingers on his hand. "What happened?"

"That piano wasn't the only thing that was played," he said wryly. "She flirted and teased, flattered me. Being so young, I had no idea she wasn't serious in those affections she seemed to show me. I also didn't realize how, when she'd pout, and demand that I only play for her, it was out of jealousy, and how she was trying to keep my abilities, which led to more jobs than I could accept, for herself.

"I discovered that one day, when I injured my wrist as I fell on an icy patch and she got upset. I thought it was because she was concerned about me. But it wasn't. She shrieked at me, accusing me of ruining her big chance that evening to perform in front of some wealthy man. We had it out then, and it turned out, she wasn't interested in me at all. Just my playing abilities. She had maneuvered herself from party to party, seeking a wealthy man to become hers.

"All along, I'd been playing my heart out, giving every inch of it to her, and she hadn't seen me as anything more than someone to get her where she wanted, before she left me behind. It shattered my heart, and took away my love of the piano. I couldn't play without experiencing all of that heartache. Each note made me think of her."

"But you still play," Samantha said, confusion in her voice. "I heard you, at the church."

Dirk nodded. "Yes. At the church. For a long time, I didn't play at all. Then one day, Gabriel saw me touch the piano as I walked past. He said he had a dream that I played, then asked, if I wouldn't use my gifts for men, would I use them for God, as He had given them to me." Dirk laughed softly, and shook his head, offering her another cookie. "That was humbling. How could I have said no to Gabriel? To God? So, yes. I play in church. But that's it."

"Would you ever consider playing outside of church?" Samantha asked.

"I don't know. Playing only in church lets me fulfill my desire to play music, but also keeps me from being taken advantage of again. Not that I think anyone here would, but it's been hard to not shake that feeling of being wanted for only one thing. What you could give another."

Dirk studied her for a moment. "That's my story. And why I feel as though I should ask you what Gabriel asked me. Will you consider using your talents for God?"

Chapter 8

Dirk watched Samantha's face when he asked the question. A range of emotions flickered over it, before she let out a deep sigh.

"I'm not sure. I need to think about that. What made you take up printing?"

He allowed the change of subject. "When I moved here, the printer before me was ready to retire. He taught me all he knew, and I found it relaxing. It allowed me all the time that I needed to think. To heal."

When she just nodded slowly, he asked softly, "I know you've not had the time you've needed to do that, but if I can help your process, please let me know."

"It would be easier if others weren't involved," Samantha told him. "Like you, I was played for a fool. However, there's more at stake than simply my pride or my heart."

He watched as she drummed her fingers on the tabletop before seeming to make up her mind.

"I might be in trouble," she told him finally, as she met his eyes.

As she explained what had happened, everything from being raised up quickly from a governess to a sought-after performer in wealthy homes, all the way to that fateful night when she'd overheard her mentor, her fiancé, was already married and simply using her to line his own pockets, Dirk found himself getting angrier and angrier.

How dare anyone take such advantage of her! His heart felt as though it might burst from his chest, it was thudding so loudly. He wasn't sure what to say, or if he even could without the intense rage he felt bursting through his words.

"So, you can see why I've been trying to keep to myself here," Samantha continued. She sighed and rubbed at her forehead. "Both because I don't want to be outed, and a scandal to erupt, but also because I'm scared Steven will find me."

"I understand," Dirk told her. "What you've told me goes no further than this room, unless it's your decision."

"That is appreciated," Samantha said, smiling at him.

He just wished that the smile met her eyes, and that the depths of them weren't filled with sorrow.

"To be betrayed by another is a pain I wouldn't wish on any soul," Dirk said.

"What might be the worst part," Samantha sighed, "is not even the idea of a scandal. Perhaps here I am safe from it. But it's that he took the thing I loved doing, and put me at risk by doing it again."

The distress in her eyes made him search frantically for a solution. "If..." He stopped, almost too nervous to say it, but when Samantha's eyes focused on his, and he saw the small spark of hope in them, he continued. "If you ever do want to sing again, then I will play for you, and you need not worry about me having any motive other than being the accompaniment to your voice."

She inhaled sharply. She looked as though she wanted to say something, but Dirk pressed on, before he could let his fear at the words get the best of him.

"I also promise to protect you. If Steven does find his way here, somehow, I will keep him away from you. I won't let him hurt you or take you back or force you into anything. I'm a witness, and will stand by you, so that no harm comes your way. I promise you that."

They stared into each other's eyes. The room was filled with a sudden tension. A thick, heavy feeling of something Dirk wasn't quite sure of. But he knew it wasn't unwelcome. The air spoke of longing, from each of them, and before he realized it, his and Samantha's hands were touching.

Not holding, no, but both on the table, their fingers curled back slightly, and those curled fingers touching the others. He wondered what might happen if he reached out a finger and ran it across her hand. Her palm. The beautiful face watching him.

Her lips parted, and he watched them intently, almost frightened to see what would come out.

At that exact instant, his door burst open, jarring them apart as they stood, half in alarm, half in guilt.

Hank filled the doorway, then faced Dirk. "A child's missing on the outskirts. The storm's growing worse. We need your help."

Moving toward his jacket as he spoke, Dirk asked, "Who? When?"

"One of the Andrews kids," Hank answered, referring to one of the farmers on the edges of Deepwater. "Betty. We go in groups of four. You're with me."

Dirk nodded, and stepped toward the door, then stopped, surprised Samantha was behind him.

"Is there any way that I can help?" she asked.

"The women are collecting at the café," Hank told her, "to help make food and have hot drinks ready for the searchers."

"Then that's where I will go," Samantha said.

As they walked outside of the shop, Samantha rested her hand on his arm. "Good luck," she told him. Then, she leaned close, and the sweetest scent of jasmine brushed against his nose. "Be safe."

Dirk nodded, and followed Hank, trying to keep his mind on the rescue, not the woman who he'd—no doubt about it—fallen head over heels for.

"This way," Hank called, and Dirk realized he'd been daydreaming and had started along the wrong path.

The child first. Then Samantha. He had to focus on the girl. "How did she go missing?"

"I'm not quite sure," Hank said grimly. "But I do know that family doesn't have much. They've had two years with very little harvest. It could be the little one was foraging for any last berries or mushrooms or tubers."

"Does Gabriel know?" Dirk asked.

"He does. He's offered them help time and time again. They always refuse." Hank shook his head. "Andrews is proud."

Though he had no children of his own, Dirk wondered if he'd be the same. A man didn't like to think he couldn't provide for his family, and accepting help was hard. Many couldn't do it. Especially when they knew who it was from.

An idea started to form, and he intended to talk with Gabriel once the child was found and he was back in town.

Because the child would be found, he was sure of it. None of them would stop searching until she was.

The snow fell faster now, and what wasn't already blanketed was coated in a thick, white beauty. Flakes fell in the small crack between Dirk's collar and his neck, and he shivered.

What of the child? The family being that poor, she wouldn't have warm clothes. Did she even have shoes? A shawl?

A shout rang out, from a distance Dirk estimated was a hundred feet away to his right. It was nearly impossible to see that far with the snowfall. A loud whistle sounded, then another.

"Someone's got her," Hank said, relieved.

They hurried in the direction of the whistle, and met up with several other men, all doing the same. Each man had white dusting their coats, red cheeks from the biting wind, but a look of relief in their eyes, shown by the lanterns they held.

"Gabriel's got her in the cabin," Peter said, rushing up to the group. "Was the rancher Duncan who found her."

A collective group of back slaps went around, and most of the men headed back toward town.

"Stop in at the café," Hank called after them. But he made no move to leave, and instead continued, Peter and Dirk with him, to the outside of the small house the Andrews family lived in.

"Let's wait a few moments," Hank said. "I want to make sure Gabriel and Duncan get back to town safely."

A minute later, the house door pushed open, and Gabriel emerged, with Duncan and one of his hands with him.

"Good work, men," Gabriel said. He looked at Duncan and his ranch hand. "Come back to the café for something warm."

"I think we'd best be getting back to the ranch before it gets much worse," Duncan answered, shaking his head. "We'll be needed there. Beck and I can make it if we go now."

"Did the other ranch hands head back to the ranch already?" Beck asked.

"Yes," Hank told him. "Mentioned they needed to be sure the cattle had enough shelter."

"Then we will too," Duncan said. "Got to protect the herd, and don't want them looking for us in worry."

Dirk watched as the two men climbed on horses he hadn't noticed, and headed for the path. Hank led the way back to town, his lantern held high. They were all silent, and Gabriel looked troubled.

He felt that way himself. Both for the child and her recovery, but also over what Samantha had told him earlier. Now that the danger to the child was gone, his mind slipped back toward Samantha.

He had meant each word he'd told her. Dirk planned to protect Samantha with all his being. Even his life, if it came to that. He just hoped that it wouldn't.

Chapter 9

The café was filled with women in the kitchen and in the dining area, as they worked together to have hot food and drinks, the fire in the dining room blazing, and a stack of dry blankets available for the searchers.

Delicious smells filled the air, and the women took turns trading off in the kitchen, so that everyone could have a break.

"You sit down for a little," Maggie said, as she walked past Samantha. "You've not rested once since you got here almost two hours ago."

"It's hard to think about doing that, when I know there's a lost child out in this weather, and a few dozen men looking for her," Samantha admitted.

Maggie's eyes reflected the worry Samantha was sure hers held. "I agree. Poor mite. I hope they found her and are on their way back."

Just as soon as the words passed her lips, a small crowd of men entered the café, and the women sprang into action filling mugs and bowls and lining them up for the searchers. Samantha glanced around for Dirk, but couldn't see him.

"Where's my Hank?" Maggie asked one of the men.

"He's with Gabriel, Peter, and Dirk," the man Samantha recognized as the shoemaker said. "The girl was found, by Duncan Marshall and one of his ranch hands. The reverend stayed for a few moments to talk to the family and see her settled in."

Maggie nodded, but she didn't take her eyes off the door until Hank walked in about ten minutes later, Dirk, Gabriel, and Peter behind him.

Hurrying over, Samantha pressed a mug of warm cider into Dirk's hand. "I'm so glad you all found her," she said.

The reverend's face was grim. "The child had no shoes. There were rags around her feet."

The café quieted as everyone listened, expressions of horror and sorrow on their faces.

"The shawl she had was thin, her clothes were worn." He closed his eyes a moment, then opened them, shaking his head. "I need to do more. Help more. But they won't take it."

"Shouldn't nobody go without in Deepwater," Maggie said, crossing her arms over her chest. "There's no need, not when any of us would help."

"I agree," Laura said. She grew a thoughtful expression, and said, "I have a plan. Perhaps."

"We're all ears," Gabriel said, moving closer to his wife.

"What if we make the Christmas program into an opportunity to also gift the children of the town a surprise each, so that no one will know who the less fortunate are."

"We can also coordinate barrels of foodstuffs and clothes to be delivered," Peter said. "We can say it was an anonymous donor."

"That's right," Maggie agreed. "I can make bread and cakes."

"I'll put together some sacks of cornmeal and flour, tea and sugar," the general store owner called out. "No one has to know."

"We'll deliver them sneaky like," Peter said. "Knock and hide."

"It's a wonderful idea," Alyssa said excitedly. "Do you think it will work? Will the families accept them, though?"

"I hope so," Gabriel said.

As the townsfolk started fleshing out the idea of their project, Samantha asked Dirk quietly, "Can I get you anything to eat? There's so much here."

"I'd be grateful," he said, and wearily rubbed a hand over his jaw. "That snow is about a foot high. It's a little harder to walk in it than you'd expect, for something that weighs so little."

"I'm sure her family was grateful she was found, and hopefully there are no ill effects to her," Samantha said, handing Dirk a steaming bowl of potato soup.

"Sometimes I forget how lucky I was growing up," Dirk said. "We never went without as a child. Always food in our bellies, shoes on our feet."

"It's easy to forget those things sometimes," Samantha agreed. "I don't know if Steven ever did it, but I had requested that part of my earnings be sent to a children's home."

"That's a noble thing," Dirk told her. "Even if he was dishonest and never did it, the intention was there, and it's no fault of yours if he misled you."

Samantha hesitated. "If I…if I offer to do something, financially, to help with this idea Laura has, do you think others will ask many questions? You know that I am trying not to bring attention to myself."

"That's a good question," Dirk told her. "I'm not sure, but I don't think so. Especially if it's for a gift for a child."

"Then that is what I will do," Samantha agreed.

Dirk said something, but over the din in the dining room, she couldn't quite make out his words.

"What was that?" she asked, leaning closer.

His eyes met hers, and she could have sworn that his cheeks, already pink from the cold, grew a deeper shade of red.

"I said, I'm glad you are here in Deepwater."

"Is that all you said?" Samantha asked, arching a brow.

"There might have been something else." He grinned.

She looked at him, and the same delicious tension she'd felt earlier in his shop seemed to surround them again. When he didn't say anything, Samantha brushed her fingers against his, and then pulled back, just out of reach. "What was it?"

Dirk looked at her for a moment. "I was wondering if you realized that your insides are just as beautiful as your outsides." He hesitated. "And I wondered how I got so lucky to get to know you."

Warmth filled her from the top of her head to the tips of her toes. "That feeling goes both ways," Samantha said. To cover the reddening of her own cheeks, she picked up her mug of cider.

She just hoped nothing would ever make her leave. This quiet little town had something that she'd miss terribly if she did have to go.

Dirk Schmidt.

Chapter 10

"This meal is delicious. Thank you for inviting me," Samantha said, as she set her napkin on the café table.

"It's the least I could do. After all, you helped me bind all of those books," Dirk told her, taking another bite of Maggie's special apple pie.

What he didn't tell her, was that he had sat there as they worked on the books, and wondered what it was that he could do to spend more time with her. As the stack of papers dwindled, he could feel the ache of missing Samantha's company in the afternoons and evenings growing stronger and stronger.

Dirk wasn't sure how he'd fallen for her so quickly, but the fact of the matter was, the more they talked, the more he grew to love everything about her. Her voice, her laugh, the little jokes she'd tell. Then there was the fact she was intelligent, interesting, curious, and unafraid to learn about things she didn't know.

He wasn't sure he'd ever met anyone like her, and was sure he never would again.

"I enjoyed it," Samantha said.

Dirk realized she'd been talking, and hoped he hadn't missed too much, as he was lost in his thoughts.

"And I appreciated your help. It would have taken me far longer to do it on my own." Dirk smiled as Samantha flushed slightly. For being such a successful woman, she was still modest, and he found it, well, charming.

"How about a small walk through town to help us digest the meal?" Dirk asked, as he pulled back her chair.

"That sounds wonderful," Samantha said. "Could we stop off at the post office too?"

"Of course," he told her.

They left the café and slowly started walking through the town. "Let's do our walk before the post office," Samantha said. Then, she laughed, "That way, if either of us gets something, we don't have to hold it long. It's quite cold out, and I'm glad for my mittens, but they aren't very good at allowing me to hold things."

"That's a good idea," Dirk agreed.

The sky was clear, perfectly blue, and the snow had all but melted. Thankfully, it was cold enough there was no mud.

"Deepwater has turned out to be far different from what I thought it would be," Samantha mused, looking around the town thoughtfully. "I'm really glad I came."

"I am too," Dirk said. Then, he looked at her worriedly. "I hope you don't take that the wrong way."

"What way would that be?" she asked him.

Dirk wasn't sure how to answer. Was she hinting that she wanted him to admit how he felt about her? But if he answered, what if he didn't get the response from her he hoped for?

"I-I..." Dirk swallowed, trying to push down his stammer.

Samantha smiled at him, and then laughed softly. She reached over and took his arm. "Is this okay?" she asked.

He just nodded, feeling suddenly nervous. She pretended not to notice, and after a moment, he relaxed slightly. They continued walking, not really with a direction in mind. Every now and then he'd steal a glance at her, and once caught her doing the same.

"I like you," Dirk suddenly blurted out.

They stopped, and Samantha turned, studying his face for a moment. "Do you?" she asked.

Dirk's chest felt tight. He was mentally berating himself for having said aloud what he'd been thinking. Why had he done that? His words seemed to freeze in his mouth. Though he was a grown man, he felt like a schoolboy, with his first crush.

"I like you too," Samantha said. "Perhaps more than like."

The thudding in his chest got louder. "You do?" he asked.

"I do," she said, taking his arm again, and they continued walking.

Neither of them said anything for a long while. They just walked, her hand on his arm, in a companionable silence.

"Do you think you could ever love someone again?" Dirk asked. "After what happened? And so soon?"

She was quiet for a moment, then nodded. "I do. Because what I felt before, when I compare it to now, doesn't seem like love. It feels more like infatuation, grown from gratitude and a young girl who was a bit starstruck, and depending on her mentor to guide her."

"I think I feel the same, when I look back," Dirk told her, after considering her words. "What I felt then, even the hurt I felt, is nothing compared to what I feel now, and the pain I suspect I'd feel if you left. That's how I know this is different. You are different."

Samantha stopped, and positioned herself in front of him. "I don't want to leave. I want to stay here." She bit her lip, then slowly added, "With you."

"I'd like nothing more," Dirk whispered, putting his hands on her elbows and stepping slightly closer. "Samantha, I—"

"Hello, Miss Lundy!"

Dirk felt gratified to see the slight expression of irritation on Samantha's face, before she fixed a smile and turned, waving to the woman who walked past.

She turned back to him with a sigh. "That was untimely."

He laughed, and started walking to the post office. "Shall we see if either of us has a letter?"

"I'm hoping I don't," Samantha admitted, as they drew closer to the post office. "But I still check. If my old music teacher found me, who is to say Steven won't?"

"It is strange how she knew," Dirk agreed, as they stepped up to the building to wait their turn. "It's a beautiful stocking she made you."

"It is," Samantha said. She grew a faraway look in her eyes. "Things were much simpler back when I was a child, having lessons with her."

"I'm sure you've nothing to worry about," he assured her. "From what you've told me, you left so quickly and quietly, it's unlikely he will ever discover where you are, and no one here knows either."

"I hope you are right," she murmured.

When it was their turn a moment later, they stepped up to the counter. Peter greeted them. "Nothing for you,

Dirk. Samantha, you've got a letter. Pretty far away too! Virginia. Family?" he asked, handing it over.

Samantha took the letter, and her face grew so pale, Dirk could see a hint of freckles on her cheeks. Concerned, Dirk led her to the small bench near the post office and helped her sit.

Samantha's eyes were glued to the envelope, and her hands trembled.

"What's wrong?" Dirk asked.

His words seemed to break into her shock, and she looked over at him. "He's found me," she whispered. "This letter is from Steven."

Chapter 11

Samantha poured herself a third cup of chamomile tea. It was supposed to calm the nerves. For her, it hadn't. They were still jangling about, just like her body had in the stagecoach to arrive here. She felt sick to her stomach. It had happened. What was she to do?

Steven had found her. Worse than that, he was threatening her. She didn't even know what manner of vengeance he would seek. It could be against her, against someone she knew—perhaps this town?

One was just as bad as the other, and she'd seen Steven angry before. It wasn't something she wanted.

Taking in a deep breath, she slowly unfolded the letter—for at least the dozenth time—and read it once more.

Samantha,

Come back. Sing again. That's all I am asking.

The woman you saw meant nothing to me. You always have been the one I adore. I have left her, and my heart belongs only to you. When you arrive, we will marry.

In case you have doubts as to my sincerity, let me make a promise that will, perhaps, entice you further.

I know where you are, and I know how to cause trouble for you. If you do not return within a week, then you will regret what you have done. You can not, will not, leave me the way that you have.

No matter where you go, you can not hide from me. My reach is far, my resources vast, and nothing will keep me from what it is that I want.

You should know this. Don't be foolish. Be a sensible girl and come home. I am waiting.

Seven days.

Steven

Fear laced with disgust filled her at his words. Then, there was anger. Somehow, it spiraled back around into worry. If he fooled the one woman, his wife, into thinking he loved only her, then he'd likely fool her too. He already had. Samantha would never let that happen again.

She wouldn't go back. Refused to.

But what of his threat? She knew her performances had made him a good deal of income. Money that he likely sorely missed now. That was the reason he wanted her to return. Not love. Not worry over her wellbeing. In fact, he hadn't even mentioned that. There hadn't been a shred of concern over her. It had all been demands. Had he always been that way? Only, she just hadn't noticed?

With a deep sigh, she closed her eyes and rubbed at her temples. When she opened them again, she drank deeply from the cooling tea, and her eyes fell upon the stocking from Miss Nightingale.

Samantha crossed the room, and touched it. Her fingers drifted over the silver trim, and the love and care and time put into its creation seeped into her soul, finding its way into each crack of her shattered heart and piecing it back together. It was just what she needed. She'd been wrong, thinking to use the stocking as a reminder never to sing again.

The stocking was a gift. A reminder of the joy which music brought to others. Had brought to her, at one point.

Resolve filled her. She would sing again. But it wouldn't be for Steven. It would be for the people of Deepwater, not for profit and comfort and ease in her life, but to bring happiness and joy to others, to use her voice to sing of the newborn, lying in a manger and the gift He would later bring to all.

She looked at the sheet music Miss Nightingale had given her, and shook her head. "How could I have been so foolish, thinking I could get away? Could hide? And why should I?"

Her shoulders straightened. "Why, I've done nothing wrong. Perhaps I have been naïve, let myself be taken advantage of, but there was innocence on my part, and now that I know—as soon as I knew—I left. Surely, that counts for something?"

She bit her lip and began to pace. "My name and reputation matter very much to me. I came to Deepwater to make a new start, and that's just what I will do. Only...what do I do about Steven?"

Her eyes fell on the letter again, and a pang of despair filled her. She felt so very alone, with a problem so large, she wasn't sure how to manage it. She only knew that she must, and that it needed to be done quickly.

There were good people here in Deepwater. She'd learned that. Surely one could help her, but who? Not the reverend and Laura. He was such a good man, he'd try to help her, and Laura was beyond sweet and caring, but they had their own worries, what with the Christmas performance and all of those families to help.

Then, there was Maggie and Hank. Samantha felt they'd be very valuable allies indeed. There was no sheriff in town, but it was clear Hank, having had some law experience, was the fill-in, and likely had suggestions. But Hank and

Maggie had a young son, and she refused to risk danger to any of them.

So, then, who? Her mind refused to even consider Dirk. She should never have even told him about what happened. Now, she'd not only fallen in love with him, but he'd admitted how heartbroken he'd be if she left, which, truthfully, would be the only sensible solution. But she couldn't do that to him. Selfishly, she couldn't do that to herself.

There was a knock at her door, and Samantha gasped loudly as she jolted. Her arms instinctively wrapped around herself. Steven! He hadn't even given her a week. Fear rooted her to the spot.

"It's me!" a familiar voice called out, and Samantha nearly collapsed with relief.

"I-I'm coming," she said, willing her shaking legs to cross the room.

Yes. It would have been sensible to leave right then. Leave and try to hide once more. Only...

As the door opened, and Dirk stood there, concern on every part of his face, Samantha fell against him with a sob. "I'm not sensible at all," she cried, and wrapped her arms around him, never wanting to let go.

Chapter 12

Dirk instinctively wrapped his arms around Samantha as she threw herself at him. He had no idea what she meant, about being sensible, but she fit perfectly into his arms and he didn't want to let her go.

His eyes closed for a moment, and as he breathed in the scent of her, he had to stop himself from resting his head on top of hers. Reluctantly, he moved back enough to see her face, and asked, "What's happened?"

"The letter," Samantha said, stepping away and brushing a hand over her anguished face. "Steven is..." She took a deep breath, then said, "He says I need to come back. Or else."

"May I see?" Dirk asked.

She nodded, and led him to her small table, where the letter was. Dirk scanned it, then read it again. When he looked up, she was staring at him anxiously.

"What should I do?" she whispered, twisting her hands. "I refuse to go back. But what trouble will he make here?"

Dirk's eyes fell to the letter once more, and he let his mind ponder her question. Finally, he said, "None. That's what."

"But how can you be sure?" she asked. "You don't know him the way I do."

"I have a suggestion," Dirk told her. "My brother is a lawyer. A good one. I will write to him directly, with your permission, and explain to him your story as you've told me, and then send him a copy, word for word, of this letter from Steven. I'll ask him to take on your case, should Steven cause problems.

"In the meantime, you can write Steven, and let him know that your lawyer is well aware of the situation and now in possession of his letter." Dirk couldn't help but smile. "Perhaps even tell him that you will not drag *his* name through the mud with the knowledge that you have, unless he persists in what he is attempting."

The smile that lit her face just then was beautiful. "What a fine idea," Samantha said. "I will write directly."

"I will as well," Dirk promised.

"I've enough paper, you can have some of mine," Samantha offered.

He joined her at the table, and the two kept their heads lowered over their paper and pencils as they wrote. Not long after, Samantha said, "I have finished. Would you care to read it, so you can let your brother know what I've said?"

"That's a good idea. Let me copy it," Dirk said.

He couldn't help but smile as he read what Samantha had written.

Steven,

I received your letter. While it might disappoint you, I will not be returning to Virginia and I also will not be marrying you.

Further, you will cease all contact with me and end your threat or you will find yourself in a situation that will be rather uncomfortable.

I have engaged the services of a very good lawyer, who is aware of both the entirety of our history and the letter you sent. He is also receiving a copy of my reply to you.

The time has passed for anything more to be said. I have no interest in associating with someone who has lied to me and makes a habit of taking advantage of others.

I'm sure the money that you have taken from me will console you until you've found someone else to provide for you.

Samantha

"What do you think?" she asked him.

"I think it's well written," he assured her. "I will see our letters get sent right away."

"Thank you," Samantha sighed. "I don't know what I'd do without you. Please, thank your brother for me as well. I'm happy to pay any fee required."

"I doubt there will be one," Dirk told her. "I'm just glad I have a way that I can help you, other than protecting you in person were he foolish enough to come here."

"I like to think he wouldn't," Samantha told him. "But who can say? Money is a powerful motivator for many."

"You are right about that," Dirk told her.

"I'm glad to see you here," Samantha told him. "And not just because you are helping me with Steven."

"Oh?" Dirk asked, curiously.

"Yes. I have something I want to tell you. Or, I suppose, ask you." Samantha stood, looking slightly nervous.

"What is it?" Dirk asked.

"I've decided to look for Laura, and tell her I'd be happy to sing in the Christmas concert for the town. I was hoping that you would accompany me on the piano."

"I would be delighted," Dirk said. "We will need to practice, and you must choose a song."

"That's already done," Samantha told him, and she walked to the blue Christmas stocking she'd hung on the mantel. "My old music teacher sent me the sheet music for 'Away in a Manger.' I will choose that."

He nodded, and accepted the music from her. "That sounds good. We will start rehearsal tomorrow."

"I look forward to it," Samantha told him.

Dirk hesitated. "What made you change your mind?"

Samantha pursed her lips. "I decided that my voice is my own, to use how I wish. I also thought about the joy that singing brings me, and how hearing a song performed well always brought happiness to me. I want to give that to others. Laura needs more people to help with the program. It would be selfish of me not to do my part, for the town that has been nothing but welcoming to me."

"I am glad that you will," Dirk told her. "I look forward to playing for you."

"Will you ever consider playing outside of the church again?" Samantha asked him.

"For the right person," he told her, looking deeply into her eyes.

Samantha flushed, and Dirk couldn't help but feel glad he'd gotten that response. "Is that so?" she asked.

"It is," he said, stepping closer.

"I wonder who that might be," she said, her voice low.

Dirk reached out and took her hands into his. "I've an idea," he told her.

Chapter 13

Samantha sat in the pew at the back of the church, watching as Dirk played "Angels We Have Heard on High" on the church piano. He was one of the most talented pianists she'd ever heard.

"I'm so glad you offered to sing," Laura said, sliding in the pew next to her. "I appreciate it. I feel like we have a good number of performers now."

"I'm happy to," Samantha said to the other woman. "Have you gotten any other offers?"

"Yes," Laura said, trying not to giggle as she brushed back some of her dark hair. "Some of the men have offered to do a little skit. They are trying to talk Gabriel into playing a role. I think that will be great fun. Of course, we will open with the children's performance and end with them as well. They've been working so hard on the play they wrote. I was thinking, would you be willing to perform 'Away in a Manger,' while the children recreate the nativity scene as the final act?"

"I think that sounds beautiful," Samantha told Laura. "What a wonderful end to the program that will make! It's properly fitting, as well."

"I agree," Laura sighed happily. "Everyone is coming together to make this just perfect. I think everyone is very excited. It seems most every place I go, someone mentions it. I'm also grateful for all of the help to bring it together. Several women are baking cookies, and we'll have hot cider along with them afterward, as we just enjoy each other's company."

As Laura continued talking about the plans for the large tree with a special gift for each child in Deepwater, Samantha realized she was looking forward to the entire event, having never done anything like it, and she was glad to be both part of the town's audience, and a performer. It was good she'd agreed. Everyone had been so kind to her here, she wanted to repay them in some way.

They still had no idea about her past—both that she was a trained singer and escaping a potential scandal. Perhaps one day they'd find out, but Dirk assured her they wouldn't care, not in the least. Why, it had only been a

Christmas or two ago there had been a shocking revelation about the reverend's past, but that hadn't stopped any of them from attending his Christmas Eve sermon.

Right after they'd locked up the highwaymen, that is.

"Music makes me happy," Laura said as she nodded toward Dirk. "I wish we had someone in town who could teach some of the children who want to learn it. Would you believe, we don't have anyone other than Dirk who can play an instrument besides a harmonica or fiddle? And no one who can teach another to sing?"

"Is that so?" Samantha asked. "I had lessons as a child, though I don't profess much skill with an instrument beyond the basics. Singing was what I loved best to do. The lessons brought me great happiness."

"I imagine so," Laura said. She let out a little sigh. "Alyssa can draw beautifully. Maggie pours her talent into baking. I wish I had a way to express the joy I felt in things."

"You help others," Samantha said. "Though you might not realize it, you have a gift for welcoming others, and making them feel comfortable. I feel joy being around you. That, for me, is a gift for me. Perhaps that is your talent. Bringing joy to others."

"Thank you for that," Laura said, squeezing, then releasing Samantha's hand. "I suppose, for a very long time, I never felt as though I had much to offer. I was sure I was bad luck, actually. When I arrived, Maggie took me in, made me feel welcome, and each time someone new comes to town, I remember how much that meant to me. How grateful I was to not feel like an outsider."

"You do a splendid job," Samantha said. Then, she touched Laura's arm. "I know I am grateful for you. You accepted me, and have fast become a good friend."

The watery smile on Laura's face filled her with as much joy as Dirk's playing music did. The two sat there for a while longer in silence, listening as he played and the children sang.

Samantha felt a warmth inside of her. A contented glow, almost. She was glad to be there, remembering the joy music brought to others, the way it could lift spirits during hardships. A flicker of hope ignited within her.

It was true, right now she had worries. Steven. He wasn't ever far from her thoughts. She was worried about a reply to her letter, but something told her everything would work out for the best. Of that, she felt sure.

Maybe it was the town's welcoming atmosphere. Perhaps it was the magical Christmas feeling in the air. Without a doubt, Dirk had something to do with it. She felt confident when Dirk was around. He'd become a good friend. And more. She just wasn't quite sure what that *more* was.

As though he could sense her thinking about him, Dirk glanced her way, and Samantha flushed. Laura, thankfully, didn't notice. Instead, she was standing and walking over to the church's door to welcome someone who had walked in. Dirk winked at her, and Samantha couldn't help but laugh as he resumed his serious expression, head bowed over the sheet music.

Later, when they walked home together, she'd tell him how happy he made her feel. How grateful she was he'd been here, protecting her, helping her, healing her. It was true. Samantha hadn't been sure she'd be able to heal when she came, she was so incredibly hurt. But somehow, she had.

She looked forward to being around him, and wondered if he'd ever consider a serious relationship with her, beyond their unspoken or hinted at words.

There was one thing Samantha knew. No matter how things turned out with Steven, if he ignored her threat and came after her, or if he simply vanished from her life, he no longer held any piece of her heart. It was entirely Dirk's, and would always be. There was no one else for her. There never had been.

She hadn't been looking for love, not ever again, but it had found her, and she knew this time that love was true. She just hoped he felt the same way about her, and that neither of their pasts would ruin what could be a blissful future.

Chapter 14

Dirk removed the paper from his printing press, carefully hanging it to dry. He'd already smudged one piece today. He wasn't anxious to have that happen again. He'd just clipped one side to the line to dry when his shop door burst open. Dirk startled, and turned.

Samantha stood there, absolute terror on her face.

"What's wrong?" Dirk asked, nearly stumbling in his haste to get to her.

"Someone's here looking for me," she gasped, falling into his arms.

"What? Who?" Dirk demanded.

"I don't know," she said, casting a frightened look over her shoulder and through the window. "I was walking back from the general store, and passing the café. You know how it's next to the stage stop?"

Dirk nodded.

"I was near, and I heard a man ask where my home was. I didn't stop to see who. I ran to come here."

Dirk felt both a rush of pleasure that her first thought was to seek him out, and also a ferocious feeling of protection wash over him. He didn't know who this individual was, but he'd keep Samantha safe, no matter the cost to him.

"Was it Steven?" he asked. Then he frowned. "Though, I'd think you'd have recognized his voice if it was him."

Samantha shook her head, the wild look still in her eyes. "I don't think so, but I'm not sure. He had a hat low over his head and a scarf wrapped around his neck and face, which seemed to muffle his voice."

She took a deep breath. "He may have hired someone to come after me. What should I do?"

"You'll wait here," Dirk answered her firmly, releasing her and giving her a small push toward his back room. "I'll go for Hank. Wait here where no one can see you."

"Should you go? What if it's not safe?" she asked, her voice shrill from fright.

Just then, his shop door opened. Dirk glanced up, frowning as a man in a scarf walked inside. He moved closer to intercept.

"It's him!" Samantha cried out. Then, she stepped forward. "Who are you? I won't go. You won't make me."

The man removed his hat and scarf, to reveal his face. Dirk relaxed at once. "My apologies. I didn't mean to upset you, Miss Lundy," the man told her. Then, he grinned at Dirk. "Good to see you, brother."

"James! What are you doing here?" Dirk asked, reaching out to pull his brother into a hug.

"I have news for Miss Lundy," he said. "I thought I'd deliver it in person, and spend a few days here with you."

"It's good to see you," Dirk said. "You are welcome any time. Though, you did give us a fright."

"And I'm sorry for that," James said. He glanced at Samantha. "After all you've been through, I should have thought to warn you I was coming. I wasn't sure my letter would arrive before me, so I just came."

"No matter," Samantha said, stepping closer. "I've quite recovered now." She twisted her hands together. "But you said you had news?"

"I do," James answered.

"Let's get you a warm drink," Dirk said. "It's colder out there than it was an hour ago. I expect the stage chilled you as well. Let's get you warmed up, then you can tell us."

In a few moments, the three were squeezed in at Dirk's small table, some slabs of a lemon cake he'd bought from the café that morning before them. Samantha poured three cups of tea. Though she was being patient, Dirk could tell she was nervous, and reached across the table to squeeze her hand.

"I'm sure all is well," he told her in a low voice.

Samantha merely nodded as her reply, though she did give him a small squeeze back, and a grateful look.

"Well," James said. "I paid your former fiancé a visit, Miss Lundy."

"You did?" she asked.

"Yes," he told her. "I also learned a good deal about him. Which is what prompted the visit." James stood and walked to his coat, retrieving a stack of papers he'd folded and placed in an inside pocket.

"Let's see," he said, as he opened the papers and ran his finger down the small writing. "Your former fiancé was quite a scoundrel. He was leading on four different women, each of whom were providing him with large sums of money. You, of course, by performing, another who was the daughter of a wealthy businessman he "consulted" for, and then two others, each with their own story of betrayal from a man they thought only had their best interests at heart. He hadn't gotten much in the way of funds from them, but had been attempting to. A fraud if ever there was one."

Samantha gasped. "I can't believe it! How could I have never known?" She shook her head as she bit her lip. "He had me completely fooled, I'm ashamed to say. What of his wife?" she asked.

"Mm, he wasn't actually married to that woman," James said, glancing up from the papers. "He'd had a ceremony, but it was never done by an official. It wasn't legal at all. He'd fooled her as well. She was supposed to inherit a sum of money. I suspect he'd hoped by pretending to be married to her, he'd have control over it."

"And by not marrying her, he was free to do as he pleased," Dirk said dryly. "Does the woman know about the false marriage?" he asked.

"She does now," James said. "Much to her relief, I am sure. So do the others. Your leaving, Miss Lundy, caused quite a stir, as they knew you were connected to him."

"I see," Samantha said, looking down into her tea. "They all must think the worst of me. Those I sang for, as well."

Dirk's heart squeezed at the soft, pain-filled sound. "No one who knows you could think that," he tried to assure her.

A small smile formed on her face, but it wasn't a happy one. "Ah, but no one really takes the time to know another, especially when they are hired to perform. They don't know the real me," she told him gently. "Very few do."

"Then I feel among the fortunate few to do so," Dirk said, saying the words even though he could sense his brother watching them closely.

James spoke then. "Though they might not, once word got around that there were women being misled by him, and how he'd been deceptive in his personal and business practices, several have said that you will be welcome again, should you wish to return to performing. I was tasked with telling you this. A Mrs. Lydell pressed me to deliver her words personally."

"Mrs. Lydell? Then it must be all right," Samantha mused. "They are an incredibly wealthy family. Whatever they say or do, others copy."

Samantha sat there for a moment, surprise on her face, and then thoughtfulness. Dirk felt worried. Scared, even. Would she return? He knew the joy that singing brought to her. It would be selfish of him to beg her not to go. Without Steven there now, she'd retain all of her money. Samantha could be a very wealthy woman indeed.

The room was quiet, the only sounds the soft snapping of the fireplace, and James's fork as it touched his plate and the cake vanished.

Dirk tried not to stare at her, but the silence—her consideration—seemed to eat away at him. What would he do if she left?

Chapter 15

Samantha couldn't remember the last time she'd been so exhausted. It wasn't a tiredness of the body, but a complete and utter weariness of her mind. Her emotions had been going first one way and then the next.

First, of course, she'd come here, hiding from Steven, wanting to start fresh. She'd been on high alert, though gradually she'd relaxed. Dirk had been part of that. It was impossible not to feel comforted, peaceful, in his presence.

Then, just as she'd released the fear she'd held, Steven found her. Once again, her emotions shifted as hope had formed when Dirk had suggested she contact his brother, but when he arrived today—frightening her half to death and bringing news that she was welcome again, if she wanted to return—her heart no longer really knew just what she wanted.

She thought she'd known...to hide. To give up music. But when she'd remembered how much joy it brought, she knew she couldn't stay away. Now, however, she was faced with a choice that she never expected.

The option to return. Be back in the spotlight, performing before others, bringing in more money than she'd ever imagined. She could. She'd be welcomed back, accepted. But that meant that she'd have to leave Deepwater. What would happen then?

She knew what would happen. She'd miss Dirk terribly. Perhaps...perhaps he'd consider going with her! Samantha smiled at the idea. Could she convince him to play for her?

The idea was exciting, bringing him into her world. She didn't need to worry about scandal attached to her name now. Her old life, with dances and fancy foods, being treated as though she was special awaited.

For a moment, Samantha let herself daydream. She and Dirk would glide across the room, she'd sing, he'd play, everyone would clap...It was a beautiful image. But that's all it was.

She glanced at the wall. Just on the other side was the print shop, and Dirk.

In her heart, she knew he wouldn't be content leaving Deepwater. Yes, he'd played the piano for others before, but she sensed it didn't bring him the same kind of satisfaction that his print shop did. He was needed here. An important part of the town.

The more she thought about it, the more Samantha realized she liked it here too. It would be difficult to go back to Virginia, to performing. The rules and expectations were so high there. So different. Here, she felt...free. Welcome. Wanted for who she was, not what she did.

"It's so hard!" she cried out, frustrated. Samantha rubbed at her forehead and tried to calm the constant conflicting emotions that filled her. She almost felt ill how they swung from one mood to the next, like a child on a swing.

Samantha sighed, and moved from her sofa to the small kitchen. "This indecisiveness will get me nowhere," she said, pouring herself a glass of warm milk. It had heated to the perfect temperature, and she put a spoon of honey in it to sweeten it.

Her eyes roamed over the small house. It wasn't just a building. It was a home. Her home. Everything from the rugs on the floor to the bare spot that would hold the painting Alyssa was making her of the town...it was something she'd put together, felt comfortable in.

And, of course, there was Dirk, just a wall away. If she were to be honest, he was the reason she was hesitant.

What would life be without him? She knew the answer to that, without pause. It would be lonely. Empty.

Samantha's eyes fell onto the stocking her former music teacher had sent her. "What do I do?" she asked it, as she walked over and rested a hand on it.

The velvet crushed beneath her brush, and Samantha traced the music notes on the stocking's cuff. Then, as clearly as though Miss Nightingale were in the room, Samantha could hear her music teacher telling her, "Listen to your heart. It will never lead you on a false path."

Samantha drew in a sharp breath. Her music teacher had told her those words before. But hadn't she always listened to her heart? And see where it had gotten her! In trouble!

But...no. That might not be entirely true. Samantha bit her lip. There had been that niggling doubt at times. She'd always ignored it...but supposing she hadn't?

There was a knock at her door, and Samantha crossed to it quickly, glad for the distraction. To her surprise, Alyssa stood there.

"Come in," Samantha said, stepping aside.

"Only for a moment," Alyssa said, rubbing her hands together. "I had a question, and it couldn't wait."

"Of course. How can I help?" Samantha asked.

"It's about the Christmas program," Alyssa said. "Laura would have come, only she was asked to help tend to a sick family. She wondered if you'd be willing to help decorate the tree with me, with the gifts for the children?"

"Oh! I'd love to," Samantha said with a broad smile. "That sounds wonderfully fun."

"I think it will be," Alyssa said. "I was going to do it this afternoon, as Christmas Eve is in two days. Will that work for you? Peter and the general store owner are bringing the toys to the church building. I was on my way there now."

"Let me get my wrap," Samantha said, hurrying over to sling it about her shoulders.

They walked to the church, talking very little. The cold was so biting, Samantha's teeth were chattering by the time they made it inside.

"Goodness," Alyssa said, rubbing her hands together. "I'm glad there's a fire burning in here."

"Me too," Samantha said, holding her hands close to it.

"These must be the gifts," Alyssa said, glancing at two large boxes.

There were small dolls, toy wagons, a drum, sacks of marbles, and carved animals like horses. Samantha kneeled next to the box. "This twine must be to put the gifts on the tree?"

"I think so," Alyssa said. "Let's start."

They worked together, hanging the children's gifts onto the five-foot tree that sat on a low table in the front of the church.

"No one will be allowed inside until Christmas Eve," Alyssa said, "so they will be a wonderful surprise for the children."

Samantha agreed. She stepped back to admire the tree. "It looks lovely. To be a child again," she laughed softly. "No worries. Well, few anyway."

Alyssa gave her a sideways glance. Slowly, she said, "Sometimes those worries and challenges we have as adults make our future better than we could have ever imagined."

"You are right, I know," Samantha sighed. "But sometimes you are stuck at a crossroads in life, and it's difficult to know which way to go."

"Are you there right now?" Alyssa asked.

Samantha nodded. "Yes." She didn't look at Alyssa, worried the other woman would see how overwhelmed she felt.

"Desperation," Alyssa said quietly, "can lead to unexpected outcomes. But that doesn't mean they are bad."

Samantha glanced at her then, listening.

"Do you know how Peter and I met?" Alyssa asked.

"I'm not sure I know the whole story," Samantha told her.

Alyssa laughed, and sat down in the first row of pews. "It all started when I arrived in Deepwater, and was rejected by my husband-to-be because my bosom was too small. I stormed off, and a short time later, Peter nearly pushed me into the stream. After that…"

Samantha listened in amazement, laughing at moments, tearing up at others, as Alyssa shared her story. An hour later, as she walked home—after promising to have tea with Alyssa, Laura, and Maggie the day after Christmas—her heart felt light.

She'd reached her decision. Truthfully, she'd known it all along. What Alyssa said about desperation leading to unexpected outcomes resonated with her. She liked that.

Life right now was unexpected. But it was good. She had a town filled with people she liked and who liked her. She had enough money that, if she was careful, would last her for a long time, and Virginia, as tempting as it was, was missing one very important thing.

Dirk.

And so, Samantha knew that her heart belonged here, in Deepwater, and with Dirk. If he'd be willing to risk love again.

Chapter 16

The church building was filled, likely beyond capacity. Small children sat upon their parents' laps, chairs were squeezed in along the sides, and a few people clustered at the back of the room near the double doors, being late and forced to stand as there were no more seats available.

Dirk sat at the front, playing soft music on the piano as everyone had squeezed into the building, and now their eyes were focused on the front as the children moved toward the small stage that had been made, ready to start the performance.

The women of Deepwater had outdone themselves—as usual—with the decorating. There were ribbons and bows in reds and whites on the pews, wreaths on the windows and doors, and extra candles along the sides. Someone had brought in some fresh pine cuttings, and it smelled wonderful.

As the program progressed, first the school children performing a play, then several others reciting poems, telling jokes, and then a trio of women singing, Dirk found his mind wandering slightly.

He could see the small girl who had been rescued, now sitting with her parents after the children's performance. Her eyes were wide with wonder at each act. He wondered how she'd feel once she saw the tree that was hidden and that would have a gift for her on it. He and Samantha had picked out something special for her, and a few other children.

Samantha. His eyes kept wandering to her. Eventually, the program grew near to the end, and Samantha rose, stood near the piano, and sang while the children formed a live nativity.

Her sweet voice was clear, perfectly pitched, and Dirk couldn't help but smile as awe filled the onlookers. It was obvious to all now that Samantha wasn't just a talented singer, but she was a trained one as well. It was evident in her posture, in the perfection of each note.

Dirk felt proud of her, proud to be playing for her, to be accompanying her in some small way. It also made him happy, because he knew that Samantha had a gift that should be shared, and he was so glad she was here tonight, using her talent for others.

As the verses to "Away in a Manger" continued, the assembled townsfolk joined in. Dirk played, but his eyes never left Samantha. In this moment, too many emotions filled him, joining with unanswered questions.

What would she do? Would she return to Virginia? She was beyond talented, and deserved to be before crowds, if that's what she wanted. Deserved to be adored, even if it was by those other than him. It would be selfish of him to want anything more than Samantha's complete happiness, even if it would make him lonely for the rest of his days.

The children portraying Mary and Joseph, along with a baby looking to be only a few weeks old, sat, and the others acting as shepherds and angels gathered around them, singing reverently.

It was heartwarming, and yet his heart and stomach felt sick. What if he never heard Samantha's sweet, clear voice again? That was all he'd been thinking about. Whether she would leave. There was only one thing to do, if he wanted her to stay. He had to tell her that. Give her a reason. But could he? Dare he be so selfish?

He had been thinking a lot about the answer to that question. What kept moving to the forefront of his mind was another question. Was he ready to give his heart away? Dirk thought he wanted to take a chance on love again, with Samantha. But, when the moment came to tell her that, could he do it? He wasn't sure if he'd fully recovered from the rejection that had once wounded him.

Dirk closed his eyes for a moment, not worried as he played, for his hands knew each key and where to position them. He wouldn't miss a note, not on this song. When he opened them a moment later, he realized there was moisture in his eyes.

Was it from his worry over Samantha's decision? His fear of losing her? The beauty of the town gathered together, watching the nativity and the children's sweet faces? He was glad to have that as an excuse, because most every other eye in the room was damp. It truly was a beautiful sight just now in the church. Gabriel, Laura, and everyone else who had worked so hard for this moment should be proud of themselves.

Samantha met his eyes just then, and Dirk almost faltered, but his fingers knew what to do, and played the final notes, letting the sweet melody drift through the church.

He loved Samantha. He knew that. It was time to let her know as well. There would come a point that if he didn't, it would be too late. He was going to tell her. Tonight. Take the risk of it. And hope that, when she did return to her life back in Virginia, for it was obvious she would as so much awaited for her there, his heart wouldn't break too badly.

Chapter 17

Laura, Alyssa, and Samantha stood before the Christmas tree covered in gifts. The children of Deepwater stood speechless, and many of their parents had eyes just as wide, several with tears in them. The little girl who had been lost, then rescued, held tight to a doll, her eyes never leaving it, her face filled with amazement.

Samantha's heart was near bursting with joy right now. Being here, witnessing this...it was something she never realized was missing in her life.

"This needs to be an annual tradition," Gabriel murmured to Dirk. Both men stood close by.

Samantha smiled. What a wonderful idea that was! She'd be sure to donate each year and—

And she might not be here next year. Or the year after. She hadn't decided yet. Too much depended on Dirk. How he saw their future. She needed to talk to him, and would try, once all of the gifts were distributed.

One by one, the last of the children received their surprises. Toy drums, carved animals, rag dolls, marbles, and more. Their smiles and excited whispers and giggles made everyone in the room feel just as excited. This was truly one of the things that made Christmas so great. Sharing joy and giving love to others.

There was a large table set up, filled with cookies of all types and jugs of apple cider and fresh milk. Everyone, adults and children alike, wandered around, enjoying the evening and eating the slowly dwindling pile of cookies.

The books that Dirk had printed had also been given out, one to each family. Samantha was sure that they would be treasured, based on the way many held them tightly to their chests. Her own was inside of her handbag, and she couldn't wait to read it later, as she sat next to her fire with a cozy cup of tea and a few cookies. It had been a wonderful idea, and would also make for a beautiful tradition in Deepwater.

If she left, would she be able to still get a copy? Perhaps Maggie would send her one. The two of them had grown close, and more than once they'd had tea together, when the café was quiet.

"Miss Lundy?"

Samantha looked down as a small girl with her top teeth missing and two long blonde braids pulled her hand back from where it had tugged on her skirt and stuck them behind her back.

"What is it, dear?" Samantha asked.

"I'm Marta. You sang just like what I think an angel must sound like," the little girl told her. "I wish I could sound and look as pretty as you do."

In all the compliments that Samantha had received over the years, something about this one—so sweet and innocent, so genuine—struck her, and Samantha decided just then. No matter what Dirk decided, Deepwater was her home. She was needed here. And needed to be here.

Suddenly, she knew just how she was meant to be here in Deepwater. Her purpose and the reason that she had ended up in the small town. But, could she really do what her heart was telling her?

"Marta, that is the nicest thing I think I've ever been told," Samantha told her. "I appreciate it more than you know."

Then, the idea she'd had magnified. All of the pieces fell together perfectly, and her heart filled with excitement. Swiftly, Samantha turned it around in her mind. Yes. She would do it.

"Will you wait here a moment?" Samantha asked the little girl. She glanced up at a woman she assumed was Marta's mother. "I want to get something to give you."

The girl nodded, and her mother looked puzzled, but nodded as well.

"Have a cookie," Samantha said. "It won't take me long, and I'll be right back."

Samantha hurried from the church. There were so many people, she'd had to weave her way through with a good number of "excuse me's" before she made it to the double doors.

The air outside was cold as it wrapped around her, and snowflakes, the perfect Christmas Eve decoration, lazily fell onto the tall pines and other trees Samantha didn't know the names of.

She walked as quickly as she could to her house over the slippery snow and unlocked the door. Once inside, Samantha strode to the mantel, grabbed the wanted item, and returned to the church.

The empty town was quite eerie. Samantha realized that absolutely everyone must truly be at the church. She hurried back, and as she opened the door, the gift of warmth pressed around her, chasing away the chill as she walked back inside. When she arrived, nearly breathless, at the table with the refreshments, the little girl's face lit up. "You came back!" she said.

"I said I would." Samantha smiled. She kneeled down so that she and Marta were eye to eye, and said, "I have something for you."

The little girl glanced at her mother, and then back at Samantha. Wordlessly, she waited.

Samantha took a deep breath. She didn't know why she was nervous, but she was. Slowly, she offered Marta the beautiful blue Christmas stocking her own music teacher had made for her. The small embroidered silver stars seemed to twinkle, and Samantha could feel the love in each stitch made, yet there was no hesitation as she held it out. The love Miss Nightingale had embroidered in the stocking wasn't just for her—it was for anyone who truly loved music. She could think of no better way to honor this gift, and the joy that music brought to others, than by giving it to this small child.

"My music teacher made this for me," Samantha explained. "Though the stocking looks empty inside, it's filled with a promise."

"What kind?" the little girl whispered, as she reached her hand forward and stroked the embroidery.

"The promise that I will give you, and any other child in Deepwater, music lessons. I can teach you to sing, I can teach you a little piano. There will be no fees for it." Samantha sat back on her heels, and watched the girl's face go from shock to excitement.

"Can I, Ma?" Marta asked, looking at her mother.

"My goodness," the woman gasped. As Samantha stood, she grabbed her hands and squeezed them tightly. "You *are* an angel, Miss Lundy. I don't know how to thank you. Marta has always longed to learn music. How can I repay you?"

"There's no need." Samantha smiled. "Come find me after the new year. I'll have something arranged then, and we will start right away."

The girl and her mother nodded, and then hurried away, the stocking tucked under the girl's arm. Just before they stepped out of sight, Marta turned her grin toward Samantha and waved. "Thank you, Miss Lundy! Merry Christmas!"

Dirk walked up to her. "That was a generous thing. Once word gets around, you may have more students than time. What made you decide to offer lessons to the children?"

"Music is a gift and meant to be shared," Samantha answered. "Perhaps, though, it was impetuous of me. I don't have my own piano, I'll have to see if the reverend will let me use this one, until I can get one of my own." She bit her lip. "I'll need to figure that out very quickly."

"So, does that mean you are going to stay in Deepwater?" Dirk asked. Before Samantha could answer, he added, "Can I walk you back and have a few moments of your time once you are ready? I need to ask you something."

There was a pinched look on Dirk's face, and his brows were drawn together. Samantha wasn't sure if she should be concerned. Her stomach constricted, but she forced a smile on her face. "Of course. Though, that sounds serious. I feel a little worried."

Dirk frowned and nodded shortly. His jaw was tense, and his voice low. "It is serious," he told her. "Though I don't think you need to worry. I think it's me who is."

As her heart sank heavily into her stomach, Samantha tried not to allow fear to creep into her. Fear that Dirk was likely going to tell her he wasn't interested in any sort of romantic attachment.

That he wasn't ready to move past the hurt the last singer had filled him with.

Chapter 18

Most everyone had left the church, and Dirk led Samantha toward the door, anxious to finally get to talk to her alone. Just as they stepped outside, Maggie called out, "Dirk! Samantha! Come join us at the café."

The older woman's bright smile and her hand on each of their arms, steering Dirk and Samantha toward the aforementioned building, brooked no argument.

It was getting dark, and Dirk couldn't see Samantha's face, but he knew his own was slightly panicked. He really wanted to speak with her before he lost his nerve.

"Everything went so well," Maggie said, chattering away as she walked them to the café, then pushed open the door.

"Sure did," her husband Hank said, and set mugs of cider on the long counter in the dining room.

"Did you see the faces on the children?" Laura asked, coming in after them with a contented sigh.

"They were a little blurry," Alyssa admitted. "I was tearing up a bit."

"I doubt there was a dry eye in the place during that final performance," Peter said, handing a mug of cider to Alyssa, then taking one for himself. "Those books are amazing. Every home should have books. Thank you, Dirk, for doing that. I know it was a lot of work."

"I enjoyed it," Dirk said. "Samantha helped me, and that made it go quicker."

"Everyone did a wonderful job. Thank you for joining in, Samantha, your voice was magnificent," Gabriel said. "Dirk, your playing was most appreciated."

"I'm going to start planning for next year," Laura said. "Can I plan for you both again to sing and play?" she asked Samantha and Dirk.

"Does that include the book?" Maggie asked, waving her copy. "I might try my hand at writing a story or a poem. I feel inspired. Perhaps I'll write an account of what happened this year, while it's still fresh in my mind."

"If Dirk is up for it?" Peter said, raising his eyebrow.

"I could be persuaded," Dirk said. "Samantha was a huge help with binding."

"Teach me how to do more, and I'll be of more assistance," Samantha answered, with a smile that warmed his heart.

"We're glad you are here," Laura told her. "Deepwater needed you."

"I think I needed Deepwater as well," she answered, and Dirk wasn't the least bit surprised to see everyone nodding, as though they understood. He suspected they did. After all, hadn't each of them come here for a different reason? Deepwater hadn't healed only him. It had comforted so many others. Perhaps that's what drew folks to this place.

As he pondered that idea, everyone gathered in chairs pulled up to the fireplace, and drank and ate their fill. They told stories, laughed, and just enjoyed being together. It felt comfortable, and it felt even better having Samantha right there.

Samantha was right next to Dirk, and he could almost hardly stand it. She was so close, but it was hard for him to not reach out and touch her, hold her hand. He wanted nothing more than to be close to her. Talk to her. Confess how he was feeling.

After a few contagious yawns, the group bade their goodnights, and Dirk tried not to rush Samantha out the door. It was finally time. They were finally alone. The problem was, it was getting late and she looked tired. He knew he was.

The even bigger problem was that he'd lost his nerve. Somewhere from the time he'd first walked into the café, and the second mug of Maggie's freshly pressed apple cider, every bit of gumption he'd had, every bit of determination, had fled like a jackrabbit getting spooked.

Samantha gave him a sideways glance. "We're finally alone," she said lightly. "What was it you wanted to talk to me about?"

He winced. Dirk couldn't help it. He'd half hoped she'd forgotten. It would have been easier if she had. Now, things felt even more awkward. She expected him to talk. To tell her what he'd been so anxious to say.

Dirk rubbed at his neck and pulled at his collar. "Ah, that is…"

He anxiously ran one hand through his hair, along his jaw, rubbed at the opposite shoulder. "I mean, well, you see…"

The night sky was open before them, the inky skies dotted in bright lights. For a moment, his mind wandered as he took in the shadows and gentle snowflakes still falling.

He wanted to enjoy this moment, but he was too scared. No, he wasn't scared. He was terrified. This was the second time he'd fallen in love with a singer. Would it be the second time he was cast aside?

Dirk started again. "Well, what I'd wanted to say…"

The words died on his lips again. He couldn't do it. He just couldn't do it. It was a strange thing, as an adult, as a man who ought not to be afraid of anything, to be near shaking in his boots. Could she tell?

Samantha stopped walking, and turned to face him. "I'm listening," she said with a smile.

Dirk was sure she was. Her sweet face was focused on him, her eyes searching his. Dirk nodded. He could do this. Would do this. There was no need to be nervous. "What I wanted to talk to you about, was us," he said, pleased the words had started to flow.

The moonlight was dim, but it was enough where he could make out Samantha's face. Now it was her who looked nervous. "Is that so?" she said, trying to smile, but failing as her voice faltered. "In what way?"

"I know you have a choice to make," Dirk said, his voice low. He forced the words out. He couldn't take them back. Couldn't contain them any longer. "To return to music, and Virginia, and your life there or to stay here, in this small town, where there's not a lot here for you. Not like you are used to, anyway. Stores, fancy parties. Crowds waiting to hear you sing." He paused, trying to sort his thoughts. "We don't have all that. We're just...simple. I know you also told Marta you'd teach her. But..."

She hadn't spoken, just waited. Dirk was both grateful for that, but also now anxious. If she'd disagreed with him, had thought that Deepwater did have something to offer, wouldn't she have spoken by now? Even interrupted him? It made him wonder if he should even continue to tell her how he felt.

And then, in an instant, Dirk made a decision. He wasn't going to tell her. He was going to spare himself the hurt. The pain. Suffering. It was Christmas Eve, and he didn't want to be associating this time of year with the loss of the woman who held his heart.

He wouldn't do it. No matter he'd started to think about love again. He'd been foolish. Wrong to do so. He'd never do it again. It would be better to live with a love he'd never professed to have, than a love that rejected him once more.

Chapter 19

Samantha was used to the feeling of anticipation. Nerves even. After all, most performers had them at some point, and she was no different. There had been those feelings of fear swirling around so hard in her stomach she felt sick, and those smaller butterflies flying up to her chest and making it tight, her throat full of constriction.

So that's how she recognized the same in Dirk. It was obvious he was feeling nervous, by the way he would start and then stop speaking.

It would be a lie if Samantha were to tell someone she wasn't at least a little nervous right now herself. But, she also knew that she had reached a decision, and Dirk wasn't aware of it. Even if what she was about to tell him wasn't going to be what he wanted to hear, she needed to say it. And then she'd continue on, living with those consequences.

"Dirk," she finally said softly. "Do you mind if I say something?"

"Go ahead," he answered, relief flashing over his face so quickly it was almost comical.

"There's been something on my mind," she continued.

Now, a strained worry formed in his eyes, and Samantha took one of his hands, as much to calm him as herself.

"I appreciate all you've done for me since I've moved here. How you made sure I was included, how you have taken care of me when I needed help, everything from a few minor repairs to the entire mess with Steven."

"It-it was nothing," Dirk told her. His eyes searched her face before he continued, "It was a pleasure to help."

"It was a relief for me," she said, starting to walk slowly. They stayed in step together. "A virtual stranger, and overwhelmed by everyone here. It was...too much at first. But you made it bearable. Enjoyable. Made Deepwater more than a town I could escape into, to find some way back to myself. It became a home."

Dirk didn't say anything, but Samantha could feel the tightness of his muscles, see it in the corners of his eyes.

"You've done so much for me," she continued, "I hate to ask. But..."

"But?" he asked, stopping them and facing her. "If it's within my power, I'd be happy to."

Samantha squeezed his hand and gave a little sigh. "You don't need to say yes," she told him. "You don't. I want you to be sure. It's just..."

She took a moment then to gaze over Deepwater. There were dim lights from candles and lanterns in the homes, and she knew that in those with children, there was excitement for tomorrow's family festivities. Right now, those children had no care in the world. She'd forgotten what that felt like.

The gentle, icy flakes that fell and coated the town reminded her that imperfect things, like her past, Dirk's past, could be hidden, but would eventually return. She could accept that. Deal with it. Move forward. But could he?

"Tell me," Dirk said, almost demanding now. "Whatever it is."

Samantha nodded. She felt resolute in her decision. "Something is missing, and I wonder if you would be willing to help me with it."

"Of course. Did you lose something?" he asked, glancing about as though it might have been a glove or her hat.

"Not exactly." Samantha took a deep breath, trying to figure out how to say what was in her mind and on her heart. "I know you were hurt before, and I was too. I wonder if because we have a mutual past, if perhaps you'd consider a mutual future."

"A mutual future?" Dirk echoed.

"Yes. With me." Samantha stepped back so she could see Dirk better. Her hands squeezed together, and then she pressed them against her stomach to quell the uneasiness that filled it. She took a deep breath, then blew it out slowly.

"I'm asking, Dirk, if you might one day have room for me and my love for you in your heart."

Chapter 20

Dirk froze in shock. The words that had come out of Samantha's lips were not the ones he'd expected. Not at all. But now that she'd said them, he—

He was wasting time not answering. It wasn't the time to think anymore. It was time to act.

Dirk stepped close to Samantha, and kissed her. Then he realized what he'd done, and backed up. "I'm sorry," he stammered. "I—"

Samantha leaned into him and gave him a kiss of her own. "There. We are even now," she teased, her eyes nearly sparkling with mirth.

Dirk grinned at her. It was a silly grin, of that he was sure, but right now he didn't care. "You mean all that you said?" he asked her, almost afraid to hear her answer.

"I do. I've grown to love Deepwater, and you. I think from the first moment we met, I'd felt something when I saw you. Perhaps that is why I kept being drawn toward you. Toward wanting to know more about you, and your printing, and to help with the books for the town."

"I was glad you did," Dirk said. "I hadn't wanted to push you. I felt something too, but I could also sense your heartache. And then when there was the chance you might return, I was devastated. I wasn't sure that I could go through another heartache."

"Well then," Samantha told him, tipping her head to the side slightly and smiling at him. "It's a good thing that you won't have to. I promise never to do that to you. It's you I want, not the skills that you have."

"And it's you that I want," Dirk told her honestly. "Not anything else but you. I can't give you all the things that you deserve, but that doesn't mean I won't try."

"All I want is you," she told him. A moment passed, where they simply looked at each other, and then Samantha sighed happily.

"This has been the best Christmas I've ever had," Samantha said. "Finding out that you love me, the program tonight, the fact that soon I'll be teaching music to children, and then the hour that we sat in the café, enjoying each other's friendship. Truly, I can't think of anything at all that might make tonight better."

"Dirk! Samantha!"

The two familiar voices called out, and Samantha and Dirk turned as one to see Peter and Alyssa in a wagon, coming up the street.

"We're going to deliver the Christmas barrels to a few houses," Peter told them.

"Maggie and Hank have gone along with Gabriel and Laura to do some others. Do you want to join us?" Alyssa asked. "Or are we interrupting?"

"Not at all," Samantha said. "I was just telling Dirk after the wonderful day today, I couldn't think of anything to make it better, but this might just." She turned to Dirk. "What do you think?"

"I think it's a great idea, and the end to a perfect day," Dirk told her.

He helped Samantha up into the back of the wagon, then climbed in next to her.

"All set back there?" Peter asked.

"Yes," Dirk said, settling the blanket in the back over their laps.

Two lanterns were hooked to the front of the wagon, creating a soft glow around them as they set off toward one end of the town.

Snowflakes fell gently, dusting the passengers in the wagon. Alyssa started to sing, and they all joined in. The time quickly passed, and before they knew it, the last barrel had been delivered stealthily, so that the family wouldn't know where it had come from, and the party was returning to Deepwater.

"There's time for one more song," Peter called from the front. "The last of Christmas Eve. Let's make it a good one."

"I know the perfect song," Samantha said, then began to sing in her sweet, clear voice.

Away in a manger
No crib for a bed
The little Lord Jesus
Lay down His sweet head

The stars in the sky
Look down where He lay
The little Lord Jesus
Asleep on the hay

The others joined in then, and the four sang together, a perfect harmony. As their voices blended into a sweet melody, Dirk couldn't help but think that this was a perfect example of the town.

Each of them blending together, perfectly imperfect individuals, but still somehow creating something wonderful and beautiful. He hoped that would never change.

Samantha might have been thinking the same, by the way she was gazing around them. When her eyes landed on his, Dirk thought his heart would burst, her look was so full of love.

The cattle are lowing
The poor baby wakes
But little Lord Jesus
No crying He makes

I love Thee, Lord Jesus
Look down from the sky
And stay by my side'
Til morning is nigh

Dirk reached over and took Samantha's hand. They held tightly to each other, as Deepwater came into view. This had been the best Christmas Eve he'd ever had, and he knew tomorrow, when Christmas morning arrived, it would be even better, for he would have Samantha right there with him.

Be near me, Lord Jesus
I ask Thee to stay
Close by me forever

And love me I pray

Bless all the dear children
In Thy tender care
And take us to heaven
To live with Thee there.

Epilogue

One year later, Christmas Eve

The last twelve months had gone by in nearly a whirlwind. Just after she and Dirk had admitted how much they cared for the other, he'd asked her to marry him.

When just days later, Dirk's brother James brought news that not only had Steven taken advantage of a wealthy woman, but one who was the daughter of a lawyer and now was being punished for his crimes, it had felt like an early wedding gift. Now, she no longer had to worry about him bothering her, and she was able to let that piece of her history stay where it should. In the past.

Maggie's niece, Carrissa, had recently moved to Deepwater and was an incredibly talented baker. She'd made them the most wonderful wedding cake, along with an assortment of pies to help feed everyone in their wedding celebration.

As she'd promised, right after the new year Samantha had started giving music lessons to the children of Deepwater. At first, she just had three students, but now, she had a dozen.

The life-changing gift of the Christmas stocking her own teacher, Miss Nightingale, had given her influenced Samantha, and she decided to make her students stockings as well, to be a gift for their first Christmas with her.

"What do you think?" Samantha asked, holding up a green stocking with a small angel stitched onto it.

"Marta will love it," he told her.

"I hope so," Samantha said. "It's fortunate that I will have a year to figure out what gifts I should make everyone next year. They won't want nor need another stocking once they have one."

"What about a song?" Dirk offered. "I could create the music, and you the lyrics, if you'd like."

Samantha set the stocking aside, and a thoughtful look came across her face. "I think that's a lovely idea. In fact, perhaps this should be the first one."

She crossed the room to the lovely white piano that had finally arrived from back East, and sat before it. Easily, her fingers played the melody to "Away in a Manager."

"What lyrics would you add to that?" Dirk asked. "I was thinking original music, though a familiar tune does always help someone to learn to read music."

Samantha didn't answer except for with a small mischievous smile. Then she began to sing.

Away in Deepwater,
I found a new home.
New friends and new family
To call all my own.

I found I was needed,
My heart filled with joy
And soon when our babe comes
Will it be a girl or a boy?

Dirk shook his head. "That's an odd song. Are you sure that's what you want for the first one? The meter might not work. I was thinking more along the lines of—" He stared at her suddenly. "Wait. Did you..."

Samantha laughed, and stood, hardly stepping away from the piano before Dirk had grabbed her in his arms.

"Do you mean? Are we? Am I?"

"Are you ever going to finish a sentence?" she asked teasingly. "I don't know. Are you?"

Dirk grinned at her then, that same silly grin that Samantha was very good at putting on his face. She wouldn't change that for anything, and then laughed, embracing him tightly.

"Merry Christmas," Samantha told Dirk as she rested her head on his chest. "And may our new year be filled with blessings."

"You are my blessing," he told her, his voice low. "I love you, Samantha."

"I love you," she answered.

Outside, snow had begun to fall, and Samantha found herself singing softly as she watched out the window.

Dirk joined her, slipping his arm around her waist. Together, they sang, their voices blending perfectly.

We wish you a Merry Christmas,
We wish you a Merry Christmas,
We wish you a Merry Christmas,
And a Happy New Year!

Stories in the Christmas Stocking Sweethearts Series

Christmas Melody: A Prequel by **Winnie Griggs**
Book 1 ~ November 17

Joy to the Cowboy by **Pam Crooks**
Book 2 ~ December 2

Away in Deepwater by **Sarah Lamb**

Book 3 ~ December 2

Holly in his Heart by **Jo-Ann Roberts**
Book 4 ~ December 3

Noelle's Christmas Wish by **Cheryl Pierson**
Book 5 ~ December 3

A Child for Christmas by **Kit Morgan**
Book 6 ~ December 4

Love Comes to Christmas by **Linda Broday**
Book 7 ~ December 4

Hear Harold's Angel Sing by **Winnie Griggs**
Book 8 ~ December 5

Merry's Christmas Cowboy by **Cathy McDavid**
Book 9 ~ December 5

See all the Christmas Stocking Sweethearts stories on the
Amazon Series Page:
https://amzn.to/3YSDf5D

Note from Author

Thank you for taking the time to read Away in Deepwater!
Could I ask for one small favor? Reviews like yours on
Amazon mean so much to me and help others to find my
books! Even just a single line means a lot!
Also...

***

Want a FREE book?
Stop by my website to get your no strings attached **FREE
book**. It's my gift to you, as a thank you for reading this
one.
www.sarahlambbooks.com

If you enjoyed this book, you'll love each of the books set in Deepwater

Read Laura and Gabriel's story, Trapped in Deepwater

Together, they are going to have to save themselves...and the town. Laura Ashborne is convinced she's a walking bad luck charm. Trying to make a fresh start, she sets out on a stagecoach to become a schoolteacher. However, the coach she's on breaks down in the middle of nowhere a few days before Christmas, and she's forced to spend an entire week in the tiny town of Deepwater.

Reverend Gabriel Sullivan wants to help the beautiful stranded traveler, and he'd determined to show her she's not bad luck. But when his dark past catches up to him, he's put into a dangerous situation, and Laura right along with him.

Can her desperate plan help him? Or will they let their past ruin the future they'd like to have together?

https://www.amazon.com/Trapped-Deepwater-Christmas-Bride-Dilemma-ebook/dp/B0C74R6NW6

***

Read Alyssa and Peter's story, Alyssa's Desperate Plan

"Yer too small on the top. I want a bigger woman."

Alyssa Moore never expected *that* to be the reason her prospective groom turned her away after one look. Now, with almost no money and no family to turn to for help, she's stuck waiting in a small town until the mail-order bride agency that sent her finds another match. She's embarrassed to seek help because that isn't her only mortifying situation, but it's all she can do.

When an upset woman finds him to ask for help posting a letter, Peter West is more than curious about her. As he learns more, he wonders...what would happen if her letter didn't post? At least for a few days. Would she consider staying there, with someone like him? He knows it's pointless. A beautiful woman like that wouldn't want a man like him.

As Alyssa becomes desperate and Peter tries to summon his courage, they'll each discover there's far more to a person than meets the eye—and that friendship and love can blossom in the most unexpected of ways.

https://www.amazon.com/Alyssas-Desperate-Rejected -Mail-Order-Brides-ebook/dp/B0CN8FKZX7

***

Read Carissa and Duncan's story, A Cherry Cheese Pie by Carissa

Carissa Porter is tired of being a wallflower. She's starting to wonder what's wrong with her. Why won't any man even look her way? About the only thing she can do well is bake, so she does just that, and tries to forget about how she'll be single the rest of her life.

Duncan Marshall wants to tell Carissa how he feels about her, but something stops him every time. After being left at the altar, he's not offering up his heart ever again, even if he senses she might be different. It's something he just can't risk. So, he continues to offer friendship, and nothing more.

When a letter arrives that may remove Carissa from his life, and put her in another's, will Duncan listen to his heart and show her that they should be together? Or is it too late?

https://www.amazon.com/Cherry-Cheese-Pie-Carissa-Holiday-ebook/dp/B0DDQJYMPT

***

Coming Spring 2025 Mail-Order Tailor

Josiah Adams seeks refuge in the quiet town of Deepwater, answering the letter for a mail-order husband. He yearns for a mother for his young daughter, Madeline, but the fears from his first failed marriage keep his heart guarded. For his daughter's sake, he'll try again, but when he arrives, the woman who sent the letter is nowhere to be found.

About the Author

Sarah writes captivating characters and clean romance that's anything BUT boring! From heartbreaking moments to heartwarming tales, get swept away in either historical or small town romance that pulls you in until the last page.

Nestled in the Blue Ridge Mountains of Virginia where she's married to her Texan husband, you'll find Sarah creating her next book, homeschooling her two boys, or volunteering in her community.